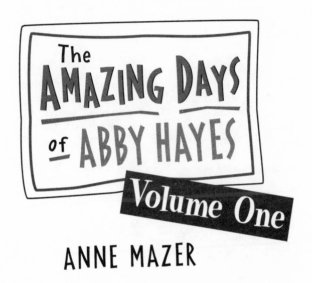

The AMAZING DAYS of ABBY HAYES
Volume One

ANNE MAZER

SCHOLASTIC INC.

New York Toronto London Auckland Sydney
Mexico City New Delhi Hong Kong Buenos Aires

Every Cloud Has a Silver Lining, ISBN 0-439-14977-0,
copyright © 2000 by Anne Mazer. Cover and interior illustrations
by Monica Gesue. Book design by Dawn Adelman.

The Declaration of Independence, ISBN 0-439-17876-2,
copyright © 2000 by Anne Mazer. Interior illustrations
by Monica Gesue. Book design by Dawn Adelman.

Reach for the Stars, ISBN 0-439-17877-0,
copyright © 2000 by Anne Mazer.

12 11 10 9 8 7 6 5 4 3 2 1   5 6 7 8 9 10/0

Printed in the U.S.A.   23

ISBN: 0-439-85375-3

First compilation printing, February 2005

Contents

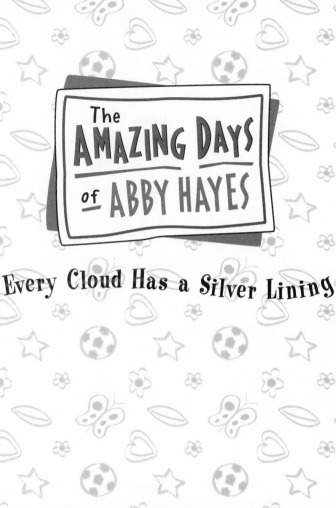

The
AMAZING DAYS
of ABBY HAYES

Every Cloud Has a Silver Lining

For Abby — of course!

How can a person be SO different from her family? I have come up with the following reasons:

1. They are aliens; I am the only normal person.

2. They are completely normal; I am the alien.

3. I was switched at birth. Some boring, ordinary family (with tangly, curly hair) wonders why they have a daughter who is so brilliant, popular, and good at sports.

4. Our family has a deep, dark secret: I was adopted.

5. What did Mom eat when she was pregnant with me?

Chapter 1

Tuesday

"He who has begun
has half done."
—Horace

Skateboarders' Calendar

Does this mean that if I start school today, I'm already halfway through the year? Yay! Hooray!

Abby opened her eyes to walls of calendars. There were big ones and small ones, glossy photographs and black-and-white drawings, calendars from many of the states and quite a few countries as well as calendars for every holiday, hobby, or interest.

Calendars greeted her every morning when she woke up and were the last thing she saw at night. The best thing about Abby's room was that she never got bored, because the calendars changed about every thirty days. Her room was like an animal that shed its skin each month to become another creature.

I have to find a World Cup Soccer calendar, Abby thought sleepily. She rolled over, turned on the light, and grabbed her notebook from the table next to her bed.

Plan for today: Do twelve sit-ups before breakfast. Run around block twenty times. (Don't stop to talk with friendly neighbors.) Eat healthy food. No donuts! No chocolate bars! Smile sweetly when Super-Sib Eva tells how she scored for her team. Nod wisely when SuperSib Isabel lectures about War of Roses. (Question: Why not War of Dandelions? Or Geraniums?) Ignore twins' fighting. Be kind to younger brother, Alex. Play chess with him when he asks. It's not his fault that he wins every game. (Be a good loser.)

Abby threw back the covers and stretched. She climbed out of bed and opened her bureau drawer. Today she was going to wear one of her favorite outfits: cargo pants and a striped tank top. She laid the clothes on the bed, then picked up a small white box that she had hidden under some T-shirts. Inside was a pair of gold hoop earrings.

Wish for today: pierced ears. How can I convince Mom to let me get them?

It was the first day of fifth grade — or, as her best friend, Jessica, put it, "the first day of the last year of elementary school." Their teacher was Ms. Kantor. She had transferred from another school in the district.

Abby picked up her journal.

Bad: I don't know who Ms. Kantor is.
Good: She doesn't know who I am. Or who my family is.

She put her journal down and walked over to her bureau. Her hairbrush lay on top of it, along with piles of seashells, rocks, and miniature plush animals. Abby pulled the brush through her tangly hair, then gazed in the mirror and sighed.

She had curly red hair that a thousand hair clips would never tame. Her eyes were gray-blue and small. Her nose — well, there was nothing to say about her nose except that it was in the middle of her face.

I have an ordinary face and extraordinary hair, Abby told herself. She would rather have had it the other way around.

She held the gold hoops to her ears and wished, for the thousandth time, that she could wear them to school. Especially today. Not only was it the beginning of the school year, but it was also the year that Abby had decided she would turn herself into a soccer star.

Abby tore off a page of her Cube of Quotes calendar.

"Every day in every way, I'm getting better and better."

Abby stared at the small, thick cube of wisdom. Why not? she thought. Why not me? I will become a top soccer player like Mia or Michelle. I will.

In the past Abby hadn't been a very good player. But now all that was going to change. Tryouts for the all-city soccer team were at the end of the week.

She stood in front of her mirror.

Think positive! Work hard! she told herself. Practice! Become a soccer star! It can happen.

She grabbed her notebook, packed it into her backpack, and went downstairs for breakfast.

"Where is everyone?" Abby asked Alex. Her brother, a second-grader, was sitting alone at the kitchen table. His hair was sticking straight up, and he had put his shirt on inside out. There was a bowl of sugary colored cereal in front of him, and he was reading a page of newspaper comics.

"You're going to turn into a comic strip if you eat that cereal," Abby warned. "Your skin will become green, and your hair will turn pink."

"Huh? Okay." Alex spooned another big bite into his mouth.

She took a box of granola from the cupboard and poured it into her favorite blue bowl. "This is healthy cereal, Alex. If you want to grow up to be a superstar like Isabel and Eva, you have to eat nutritious and wholesome foods."

Her little brother ignored her. He didn't need to grow up to be a superstar; he already was one. Probably all those pink and green food colorings had mutated his brain into its present genius state.

Abby opened the refrigerator. "Where is everyone?" she asked again.

"Eva's swimming. Isabel's upstairs reading her history book. Dad's been in his office since six A.M.," he recited.

It was only eight o'clock in the morning, and most of her family was already hard at work? What was wrong with them? Or her?

"Good morning, Alex and Abby." It was their mother, looking elegant in a navy business suit and a pale silk blouse. Her hair was gathered up in a bun, and she wore a gold necklace.

She kissed Alex on top of his head and gave Abby a quick hug.

"Mom, what's the Working Woman's Wisdom word of the day?" Abby asked.

Her mother put her briefcase on a chair. "Didn't look at it this morning, honey. I've been busy reviewing a case. Tonight I won't be home until late, but Dad will be here." She grabbed a bagel, smeared some butter onto it, and wrapped it in a napkin. "I'm late! Have to run!" She picked up her briefcase and blew Abby and Alex a kiss. "Wish me luck! I'm in court today!"

"Luck! Luck! Luck!" Abby and Alex chimed. It

was their ritual chant for their mother whenever she had to appear in court.

Their mother smiled at them one last time and disappeared out the door.

Alex's head sank downward again as he continued to read the comics.

A normal day begins in the Hayes household. Everyone is up and about at the crack of dawn except for Abby Hayes, who remains in the dream state.

"Alex and Abby!" said their father, padding into the room in pajamas and slippers. "Good morning to all!"

"Dad, you're not dressed!" Abby pointed out.

"That's one of the advantages of working at home." Her father yawned and rubbed the stubble on his chin. "Roll out of bed, grab a cup of coffee, and be at work at the computer five minutes later. And, of course, spend more time with my children," he added.

"You two have ten minutes before you have to leave for school!" He patted down Alex's hair.

"Whoa, boy! That hair is galloping off your head this morning. And let's put on your shirt one more time. You must have gotten dressed in your sleep!"

He kissed Abby. "Writing in your journal, hon?"

Of everyone in the family, Abby felt closest to her father. She wondered if she could confide in him about her soccer dreams. Maybe. Or maybe not. After all, he, too, was one of the wonderful Hayeses. He owned his own computer business, designed Web pages for his clients, and set them up on the Internet. He took care of a lot of the household chores, too. In addition, he coached Eva's lacrosse team and helped Isabel train for debates.

Her mother was a lawyer, the mother of four, a marathon runner, and she sat on the board of several community organizations.

Her brother, Alex, was a math and computer genius.

Her twin sisters, Eva and Isabel — oh, forget it!

Just thinking about what any one member of her family did made Abby feel small and insignificant. She hoped that someday she could prove that she was deserving of being a Hayes, too.

Chapter 2

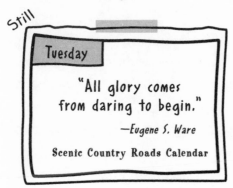

Still

Tuesday

"All glory comes
from daring to begin."

—*Eugene S. Ware*

Scenic Country Roads Calendar

Or being forced to begin.

I wish we could just skip fifth grade
and go straight to middle school.

Abby looked at her list of school supplies.

**List of school supplies needed for Ms.
Kantor's fifth-grade class:**

Pencils boring!
Pens, blue and red Why not green and
red? Or purple and orange? Brought my

favorite purple pen to school anyway.
Purple rebellion!

Crayons NO! No! I am tired of
coloring. I have been coloring since age
two. No more coloring with crayons —
P-L-E-A-S-E!!!!

**Paper, two-pocket folders, ruler, pencil
sharpener** ho hum, supplies as usual

A box of tissues Will we be crying?

List of supplies I wish we
needed:
Rainbow pens
Souvenirs from vacation
(seashells, calendars,
rocks . . .)
Lined paper in fluorescent
colors
Favorite books
CDs and personal stereos
Earrings for all girls

"Let's go around the class and introduce ourselves," said Ms. Kantor. "Let's start with me. I'm
Ms. Kantor, your fifth-grade teacher. Last year I

taught at Swiss Hill Elementary. I have two children. My hobbies are astronomy, canoeing, and speaking French."

Abby sat in the row across from Jessica. Her notebook was on her lap.

Ms. Kantor's hair is dark blond. Her nose is pointy. I can't tell if she's going to be nice or not, but so far she's okay.

"My voice may give out later today," Ms. Kantor said. "This happens every year during the first week of school. I have to get used to talking in class!" She cleared her throat.

Ms. Kantor is wearing a "teacher's dress." One of those long, flowy things. My mother looks better in her suits. She also never looks tired or flushed, and she never clears her throat. Maybe it's easier to spend all day with criminals than with kids. That's what my mother said after the school open house last year. What did she mean? I pointed out that probably some of these kids would grow up to be criminals. Ha-ha. I wonder who?

Ms. Kantor cleared her throat again. Abby hoped that she wouldn't do this all year long. One week was going to be bad enough.

"Who's next? Say your name and tell us something about yourself."

Brianna stood up. Her toenails were painted glittery orange. She was wearing bell-bottoms and a velour T-shirt. "I'm Brianna," she announced, tossing her hair like an actress on a soap opera. "I love horseback riding, soccer, and dancing."

Brianna Brag Ratio: One brag to two sentences. (Usual Brianna Brag Ratio: Twenty brags to one sentence.)

"Yay, Brianna," Bethany said, then stood up. "I'm Bethany, Brianna's best friend." She sat down again.

"Can you tell us a little more about yourself, Bethany?" Ms. Kantor asked.

"I like to ice-skate, and I have a hamster," Bethany

said, pulling at her earrings. They were tiny silver skates that dangled from her ears like charms.

Bethany is Brianna's personal cheerleader. She dresses like Brianna, looks like Brianna (except hair is blond, not dark), and acts like Brianna. Who says that science has not yet cloned a human being? They haven't met Brianna and Bethany!

Zach and Tyler stood up at the same time. "We like electronic games and computers," they chanted in unison.

"They're cute," Brianna whispered loudly to Bethany.

"No Game Boys in school," Ms. Kantor warned, pointing to Zach's backpack.

No Game Boys in school???!!! Z and T are going to be miserable. Last year they brought their games every day to play at recess and after school. If they have to leave them at home, they will wither and sicken.

P.S. Did I hear Brianna say that Z and
T are cute? Ugh!!! What is so cute about
them? They are loud, dumb, and obsessed
with technology!

The other students introduced themselves in turn.
Meghan and Rachel had gone away to sleep away
camp. Jon had played basketball and visited Norway
with his family.

There was a new girl in the class. Her family had
moved to town just a few weeks ago. Her name was
Natalie. She was small and thin, with short dark hair.
"I like to read," she said in a quiet voice. "My favorite books are the Harry Potter books. I've read
them each nine times. I also have a chemistry set. I
like to do experiments."

As she sat down, she caught Abby's eye and smiled
quickly, then looked away.

New girl seems nice. Not loud and bragging
like Brianna and Bethany. Maybe she wants
to eat lunch with Jessica and me. Wonder if
she has good dessert to trade? Note to self:

Must stop thinking about desserts! This is not the way to become a soccer star!

It was Jessica's turn. For the first day of school she had worn overalls and a black tank top. She had pinned peace signs and little hearts all over the overall straps. Her hair was in a ponytail.

She pulled out a photo of a spaceship. "This is what I want to do when I get older," she said. "I plan to be an astronaut. I also have asthma, love apricot jam, and Abby is my best friend."

"Very nice, Jessica," Ms. Kantor said. "Next?"

Abby jumped to her feet. "I'm Abby!" Suddenly she couldn't think of a thing to say. That she had a calendar collection? Too weird. That she wanted to be a star soccer player? Not yet. That she had three SuperSibs? The less said about them the better. Who was she, anyway?

"Um, my best friend is um, Jessica. . . . Um, this year my parents are, um, letting me, um, bike to the store by myself. . . . I love to write!" she finished in a burst of inspiration.

Ms. Kantor cleared her throat. "All right, thank you, Abby. I'm looking forward to getting to know you all very well. Now let's go over the classroom rules." She wrote on the blackboard:

Raise your hand to talk.
Respect others.
No hitting.
No bad language.
Turn in homework every morning. If you forget to
bring it in, you must make it up at recess.

Abby exchanged glances with Jessica. Same rules since kindergarten! Except for the one about homework. She wanted new ones. She picked up her journal.

> <u>Abby's Superior Classroom Rules</u>
> Stand on your head to talk.
> Once a week, all students speak gibberish.
> No sneakers worn backward.
> Pink is forbidden.
> Earrings required. Or parents will be sent to principal's office!

She slid her notebook over to Jessica. Her best friend sketched a picture of Brianna upside down, with a speech balloon coming out of her mouth. It said, "Blyzzzenfloobenpolk."

The two girls began to laugh.

Ms. Kantor clapped her hands. "Pay attention, everyone!" She consulted her chart. "Abby? Jessica? Settle down, now. Fifth grade is a very important year. It prepares you for middle school, where you will have much more responsibility."

Abby and Jessica looked at each other and sighed.

"Grade school as usual," Abby muttered. Now that she was in fifth grade, she knew the routine all too well. After all, she had been in this school since kindergarten.

She wished she were eleven. She wished she were in sixth grade. She wished she were in middle school, changing classes every hour. She wished she had pierced ears like a lot of the other girls in fifth grade. She wished she were a soccer star.

"I have a very exciting thing to tell you," Ms. Kantor was saying.

Abby came out of her dream. Exciting? Fifth grade? She didn't think so.

"This year, for this class only, we are going to have a special workshop every week. A friend of mine is coming to give you —" She cleared her throat.

"— a creative writing tutorial."

Abby sat up straight in her chair. She had never had a creative writing class before.

"The teacher's name is Ms. Bunder, and she will be coming every Thursday morning."

Brianna raised her hand. "A poem of mine was published last year." She glanced over at Zach and Tyler to see if they were listening.

Abby nudged Jessica. Brianna, a poet? What did she write, rhymes about her horse?

"How nice, Brianna. Maybe you can bring it in. It's quite a coincidence, but Ms. Bunder is a published poet as well."

Ms. Bunder was a published poet! Abby could hardly wait! What would they write? Stories? Essays? Chapter books? Whatever it was, she was ready.

"Maybe fifth grade won't be so bad," she said to Jessica.

"I hope Ms. Bunder doesn't clear her throat as much as Ms. Kantor!" Jessica whispered back.

Abby didn't care if Ms. Bunder cleared her throat one hundred times a minute. Writing was Abby's favorite subject — and they were going to have a class every week. Thursday was only two days away!

Chapter 3

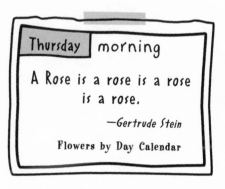

Thursday morning

A Rose is a rose is a rose
is a rose.

—Gertrude Stein

Flowers by Day Calendar

Roses are red,
Violets are blue,
My siblings are geniuses,
I wish I was, too.

        – original poetry by Abby Hayes

Roses are red,
Violets are blue,
Eva's a star athlete,
I'm gonna be one, too.

        – a poem by Abigail Hayes

Roses are red,
Violets are blue,
I'm sick of this poem,
You probably are, too.

                              — verse by A. Hayes

Who is Ms. Bunder? The eager crowd of students milling about the playground before school has nothing else on its mind. The excitement is nonstop! Some sample conversations overheard by our roving reporter:

Zach: "When you come over to my house after school, we can try out the new game."

Tyler: "I heard the graphics are great!"

The reporter moves on in search of better conversation.

Brianna (loudly, near Z and T): "The Hotshots are performing at the farmers' market on Saturday. I'm doing a solo number."

Bethany: "Yay, Brianna!"

Okay, let's try again. The roving reporter eavesdrops on another conversation.

Natalie: "Mumble, mumble . . .
Harry Potter . . . mumble, mumble."
   Jessica: "When I'm an astronaut . . ."
   What is wrong with today's fifth-
graders? They are not dying with
curiosity about Ms. Bunder's creative
writing class! Ms. Bunder's name is
not on all their lips! They are acting as
though it's school as usual.

9:02 A.M.:	Only one hour and fifty-eight minutes until creative writing.
9:04 A.M.:	One hour fifty-six minutes left.
9:15 A.M.:	We must do math. Distraction. Thank goodness!
9:37 A.M.:	Finished math in record time.
9:44 A.M.:	Ms. Kantor returns math sheet to me. All problems must be redone. "What is on your mind, Abby?" she said.
9:45 A.M.:	Reworking math problems.

10:05 A.M.:	Still reworking math problems.
10:14 A.M.:	Spelling books out. Distraction!
10:30 A.M.:	Finished spelling in record time.
10:35 A.M.:	Ms. Kantor returns spelling to me. All words must be rewritten.
10:42 A.M.:	Rewriting spelling words.
10:57 A.M.:	WHERE IS SHE??????????
10:58 A.M.:	Someone has walked in the classroom. But I don't think it can be Ms. Bunder. She is too young. She is too pretty. She is wearing bell-bottoms and a silky dark blue T-shirt. I love her sandals! They are black platforms. Her necklace is great, too. It is silver with blue stones. I wonder who she is? Ms. Bunder's college-age

daughter? Here to help
Ms. Bunder?

Abby slid her journal into her desk and watched the young woman put down a stack of brand-new notebooks. Then she glanced at the door for a sign of Ms. Bunder's arrival. She still wasn't here.

The young woman clapped her hands for attention. "Good morning, everyone!"

She was definitely too young to be Ms. Bunder. In fact, she didn't look much older than Eva and Isabel. Abby hoped that she wasn't a high school student who knew the amazing Hayes girls. It was bad enough having twin overachieving ninth-grade sisters, one with a straight A average and president of her class, the other a star of every sport imaginable. Did people have to expect the same from Abby?

Where was Ms. Bunder?

Jessica leaned toward Abby. "I like her outfit," she whispered.

Even Brianna, first in the fifth grade to wear colored lipgloss and paint her toenails, was eyeing her enviously.

"I'm very excited about this class!" the young

woman said. "We're going to do lots of wonderful writing together."

"Is she Ms. Bunder?" Abby said in shock. "She can't be!"

"She looks nice," Jessica said. "Whoever she is."

"Do any of you keep a journal?" Ms. Bunder asked.

Abby raised her hand.

"Great!" Ms. Bunder smiled at her. "Does anyone write poems or stories?"

Brianna's hand went up like a rocket. "I've published a poem," she said. "In my family newsletter."

Tyler raised his hand. "I've written a story about a kid who gets lost in a computer." His face reddened. "Zach helped me."

"Wonderful!" Ms. Bunder said. "I'm glad that some of you already write for pleasure. I want everyone to enjoy this class."

Abby and Jessica exchanged glances. Ms. Bunder's class seemed promising already.

"We're going to do a lot of writing this year. We'll be working on stories, poems, and articles, as well as writing in a journal every day."

She picked up a notebook. "I've brought one for

each of you. We'll start immediately."

Brianna whispered something to Bethany. Tyler looked pleased.

"I have lots of ideas to get you started!" Ms. Bunder took some chalk and wrote:

School Year Resolutions. Dare to Dream! What do you want to achieve this year?

Summer Summary. Your best and worst memories of the summer.

Tell me about yourself. Who are you? What do you look like? What do you love to do? Write about your family and friends.

Ms. Bunder paused. "These are just a few ideas to get you going. Choose one and write three paragraphs or more in your new notebook. I'll check them regularly."

She walked up and down the aisles, passing out the notebooks and exchanging a few words with each student.

"Abigail Hayes." Ms. Bunder stood in front of her, holding out a purple notebook.

Abby's name was written in purple letters on a laminated card on top of her desk. Had Ms. Bunder realized she loved purple from looking at the name card?

"Do you like to be called Abigail or Abby?" Ms. Bunder asked.

"Everyone calls me Abby. Except my grandmother."

"Grandmothers have their own rules," the teacher said. "Mine used to call me Violet, after a friend of hers. My real name is Elizabeth."

"You look way too young to be a teacher!" Abby blurted. "I bet they made you show your teaching ID when you arrived in school."

Ms. Bunder laughed. "The secretary looked like she wanted to!"

As Ms. Bunder moved on to the next student, Abby pulled out her old journal. It wasn't purple like the one Ms. Bunder had just given her; it was black-and-white and written all over. She was almost on the last page.

She raised her hand. "Ms. Bunder, can I finish my old journal before I start the new one? And can I write in purple ink?"

"Yes and yes," Ms. Bunder replied. "Double positive."

"I'm going to write about electronic games!" Tyler

announced.

Brianna had written in large pink letters: "Brianna, hotshot dancer and future captain of the soccer team." She drew a little heart over the "i" in her name.

Abby opened her old black-and-white journal.

Ms. Bunder's family lives near Ms. Kantor's, and she used to baby-sit for Ms. Kantor's son and daughter. Then she went away to college and decided to become a teacher and a writer. She has published poems and short stories and led creative writing workshops. We are the first elementary class she has ever taught!

Ms. Bunder has not cleared her throat once!

She laughs at jokes.

She *makes* jokes!

We can use any color ink. "No invisible ink," was all she said. (Ha-ha. I wonder who would have tried that! Probably Zach or Tyler.)

"Double positive" for creative writing class and Ms. Bunder!!

Abby opened her new notebook and wrote at the top of the page,

New Improved Purple Journal.

Around her was the sound of pens scratching on paper and pages turning. In a few moments, she was so busy writing that she didn't notice it anymore.

Chapter 4

Friday

"To dream the
impossible dream . . ."
Making Moments Count Calendar

That song is from some play my mother is
always talking about. She sings this stupid
song all the time. It's annoying. I can't
get the words out of my head.

Is soccer an impossible dream or a
possible dream? I must make myself into
Somebody. Otherwise I will be Nobody.

<u>Abby's Soccer Goals</u>
Turn myself into a great player. Soccer is
one of the few sports that Eva (SuperSib,
Super Athlete, and twin of Super Student
Isabel) does not play.

How fast can I do it? Can I do it in six weeks?

Must train.

Eat healthy foods (no more potato chips).

Read sports section of newspaper.

Pick up tips from successful players.
START TODAY! DON'T DELAY!

(Does this mean I have to sacrifice the brownies that Alex and I made to a Greater Cause? Sigh. I packed two in my lunch. Maybe I will offer one to Jessica and one to the new girl, Natalie. A welcoming gesture.)

<u>Other Goals for the Year:</u>

Do math homework right away so seven-year-old genius brother, Alex, will not find it and do it in seconds.

(He's not trying to show me up; he's just bored with second-grade math! Too bad he can't do Eva and Isabel's math assignments yet. That would show them. Ha-ha.)

Get ears pierced.

Never eat lima beans again.

Something About Me:

I love calendars. (I have seventy-three.)
My favorites are:
– an "Abby's World" calendar that my father
made on his computer. It features pictures of
me as a sunflower, in a stroller, and dumping
pots of water on Jessica at age five.
– a Spuds calendar
– the Calendar Lover's calendar that I
made, using my father's digital camera. I
took pictures of my walls as they changed
every month and made a calendar from
them! Ha-ha! I bet no one else ever
thought of doing that!

I think I am going to love creative
writing class! I'm glad Ms. Bunder's name
is Elizabeth, not Violet. I'm glad I'm
called Abby, not Abigail. Abigail is too
old-fashioned. It sounds like someone who
lived during the Revolutionary War and sat
in her parlor sewing all day. I hate sewing!
Thank goodness I live today and not then!
And thank goodness Ms. Bunder isn't a

teenager! She graduated from college, so she must be at least twenty-two. She doesn't know my SuperSisters, either. I'm the first Hayes she has met. She said she might call me "Purple Hayes" because I like purple so much. "Purple Haze" is the name of a famous song from the sixties. Ms. Kantor says she remembers it.

Summer Summary

The Hayes family went to Vermont. SuperSib Eva biked up and down mountains with friends. SuperSib Isabel talked nonstop about Hundred Years' War. (Known to fifth-grade sister as Hundred Years' Bore.) SuperSib Alex designed computerized robots without computer. Mother read legal briefs and visited antique stores and historic towns. Father drove car, made bad jokes, and introduced self to new business contacts.

Abby Hayes purchased Fences of Vermont calendar, some maple syrup candy, and salt and pepper shakers in shape of cow.

Friday evening.

After school today, we had tryouts for the all-city soccer team. Mr. Stevens, our gym teacher, will be the coach. He says no one who wants to play soccer will be excluded. Anyone can join the team if they are willing to improve.

Mr. Stevens is nice. He never yells at kids who aren't good at sports. He tries to make them feel good about what they can do.

Encouraging pat on shoulder when I passed ball to wrong person.

"Keep up the good work, Abby" when I kicked ball out-of-bounds.

"Good try!" when I missed ball completely.

Am apparently lacking in natural talent. Will have to work hard to become soccer star.

Brianna has unpleasant habit of shrieking when person misses ball or passes to wrong team.

Natalie (new girl) agrees about Brianna.

Rachel and Meghan are very good soccer players; so is Jessica, even though she has asthma. Jessica says she will definitely join all-city team. I will, too. It is my only chance for stardom.

Best friend, Jessica, has offered to help me work on soccer skills this weekend. I want to improve before practices begin at the end of next week.

Using power of mind, I will transform myself into great athlete.

(Note: Does my handwriting reveal bold determination and an unstoppable desire to succeed? Check Jessica's handwriting analysis book.)

Why does "power of mind" make me think of superhero commercials? Will I become overmuscled cartoon? Probably not. Arms too skinny.

Went home and ate plate of cookies to celebrate decision to turn self into great athlete.

Chapter 5

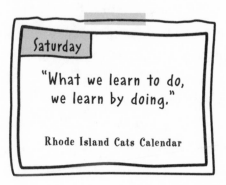

Saturday

"What we learn to do,
we learn by doing."

Rhode Island Cats Calendar

What if we don't learn anything from doing? What then? *Huh?*

Bought World Cup Soccer Calendar with weekly allowance. Put it on wall across from bed. Will see soccer players first thing in morning when I open my eyes.

Read sports page today, searching for gems of wisdom. Learned that some professional athletes train eight hours a day or more!!!! This inspires me to practice without cease.

Abby kicked the soccer ball up the porch stairs for the one hundred and twenty-third time. It smacked against the door, widening the hole in the screen. It had been a tiny hole when she began her practice. Now it was not so tiny.

Abby hoped no one would notice.

The ball dribbled down the stairs and into the bushes. Abby sighed. She had crawled into the bushes many times already. There were scratches on her arms and legs to prove it.

She sat down on the steps and rubbed her foot. It was sore. She wondered if she was kicking the wrong way. Maybe soccer cleats would help.

Jessica was coming over soon to practice with her. She had promised to show her juggling, heading, and passing.

It sounded mysterious and difficult. Abby hoped it was more fun than kicking a ball up and down the stairs.

She picked up her journal.

Must keep up positive attitude. Or all is lost.

The early bird gets the worm.

I do not eat worms! Even fried ones.
Also dislike getting up early.

Try another slogan.

The little acorn grows into a
mighty oak.

I will be like the acorn.
Future greatness now unseen.

But what if someone kicks
me onto a concrete sidewalk? Or if a squirrel
eats me? Or if I never fall off the tree?

The little rip in the screen door grows
into a mighty tear. Will family accept this
as excuse?

"Hey, Abby!" It was Jessica. She was wearing soccer cleats and shin guards and a new yellow jersey. Her inhaler was stuck in the right pocket of her shorts. She was dribbling her soccer ball. "What are you writing?"

Abby put down her notebook. "Inspiration from my mother's Working Woman's Wisdom word of the day."

Jessica raised an eyebrow. She and Abby were always reading, but Jessica read science fiction and fantasy, not her mother's daily calendars. Abby guessed she might be the only girl in fifth grade who read calendars in her spare time. She hoped that was nothing to worry about. She already had plenty of things to worry about — like her wild, tangly red hair, her brilliant and athletic family, and the soccer team.

"Ready to practice?" Jessica asked.

"Sure. Why not?"

Jessica kicked the ball to Abby. It whirled through the grass and landed in front of her.

Abby stared at the ball. What was she supposed to do now? Dribble it? The word made her think of babies drooling. She imagined someone teething on a giant soccer ball at the end of a pacifier.

"Now pass it back to me!"

The ball flew through the air. Jessica kicked it with her knee. "That's called juggling," she said. "The ball doesn't touch the ground. You can hit it with your knees or chest or head."

"What if you played with oranges?" Abby asked. "Like real juggling? If the orange was overripe . . . squish! Orange juice!"

Abby thought of Brianna with orange pulp dripping down her face. It was a good thought, even more inspiring than the one about little acorns. She would try to remember it when Brianna was screaming at someone on the field.

"Kick it, Abby!" Jessica yelled. "Get it into the goal! That's it! Keep moving!"

Abby abruptly stopped in midkick. Three people had come into the yard: her seven-year-old brother, Alex, and her twin fourteen-year-old sisters, Isabel and Eva. They were all staring at her. She hoped they hadn't been there long — especially the twins.

Alex gazed admiringly at Abby. He loved whatever she did, no matter what it was, even if he could do it better.

Alex wasn't an athlete, but he knew every strategy for every computer or electronic game invented. Abby thought of him as her secret weapon. Someday, when Tyler and Zach were just too much to bear, she was going to introduce them to her little, skinny, second-grade brother. He would beat them at any game they could name.

"Soccer?" Eva asked. She had a firm chin, firm, well-defined muscles, and a firm belief in her own excellence. She excelled in basketball, skiing, swimming, rowing, softball, and lacrosse. Even though she was only in ninth grade, she had already been encouraged by professional scouts.

Eva wore tailored shorts and a clean, ironed T-shirt. Her dark hair was pulled back into a bun. She wore no makeup or jewelry.

In contrast, her twin, Isabel, wore her hair loose and flowing. Her fingernails were painted blue. She wore gauzy shirts, long velvet skirts, and metal chokers. No one would ever mistake her for Eva!

Isabel was the top student in her grade and loved by all teachers. When she walked into a room, everyone stared at her. She had presence, charisma, and brains. She hated sports as much as Eva loved them and was constantly arguing with her twin about the value of brain versus brawn.

Isabel and Eva were rival powers in the Hayes family. They were equal and very separate. Someday one or both of them would rule the universe — but there'd be a huge battle to divide it up first.

"Sports!" Isabel exclaimed scornfully, firing the first round in the latest skirmish. "A bunch of sweaty people chasing a little ball and getting excited about it."

"Oh, yeah?" Eva shot back. "At least I'm not flabby and cross-eyed and permanently glued to the computer."

"Better than being a mindless muscle machine!" Isabel snapped.

Abby rolled her eyes at Jessica. "Here they go again," she mouthed.

In the heat of the battle, Isabel liked to say outrageous things to get her twin angry. Eva wasn't much better.

"Ridiculous!" Eva said. "Don't listen to her, Abby. Are you going to join the soccer team? It would be great for you."

Abby hesitated. She didn't want to be used as a missile in the ongoing War of the SuperSisters. She especially didn't want to tell them what she was doing.

One day she would stun them, impress them, and awe them with her soccer talents. But not yet. They would see her at the height of her glory, not in her little acorn phase. Once the power of her mind kicked in, they'd never laugh at her again.

"I'm not going out for the team!" Abby lied. "I'm only helping out Jessica."

She smiled widely. "Right, Jessica?"

Jessica looked down at the ground and didn't reply.

Abby's best friend hated lies, even little ones. But it was too late to take the words back. Abby hoped that Jessica would understand when she explained later.

"I'm going to research a science paper on the Internet," Isabel announced, dropping the argument suddenly. She gave Eva the superior smile of the straight-A student and disappeared into the house. Alex scampered after her.

"I've got an hour before my practice," Eva said. She was golden brown from her summer bike trip in Vermont. "I'll give you a few soccer tips, Jessica and Abby."

Abby stared at her in shock. That was the last thing she needed — bossy, perfect, know-it-all Eva pointing out all her mistakes!

It was just like her to butt in. Eva always showed up to show her up.

Eva tightened her sneaker laces, then straightened up. "What are you doing?"

"We're practicing passing," Jessica said. "Wanna play?"

Abby's jaw dropped open. If it hadn't been hinged to her face, it would have fallen off completely.

Jessica knew how Abby felt about the SuperSibs! And here she was, asking one to join the practice! Never mind that Eva had already invited herself in — how could Jessica be such a traitor as to welcome her?

"If Eva's here, you won't need me," Abby interrupted.

Jessica gave her a dirty look. Abby glared back at her.

"Here, Eva!" Her best friend dribbled the ball to her older sister.

How insensitive could she get?

"Watch out! Your guard is on your tail!" Eva cried.

Jessica ran, kicking the ball.

"Come on, Abby, show a little initiative!" Eva called in a loud, bossy voice. "Get the ball away from her!"

Abby ignored her sister. She headed in the opposite direction.

Eva frowned. "What's her problem?" she asked Jessica.

"Who knows!" Jessica said.

"I don't get it." Eva stared at Abby for a moment, then shrugged. "I guess we can't play today. Sorry, Jessica. Another time, maybe." She went into the house.

Jessica caught up with Abby. "You shouldn't have lied!" she said furiously. "See what happened because of it?"

Her best friend rarely lost her temper. Jessica was calm and cool in almost every situation. Her room was neat and so was her mind.

"Why did you invite her to play?" Abby cried. "You know how obnoxious Eva is about sports!"

The two girls glared at each other.

Without another word, Abby turned and stomped up the back stairs. She didn't need her SuperSis Eva butting into her life — or her best friend, Jessica, either!

She'd work out her own training program.

Chapter 6

> Sunday
>
> **"Effort is like the rain that waters our gardens."**
>
> —Mega-Muscles
>
> **Daily Inspiration Calendar**

Huh? Do I need rain? No! It would make the ground soggy and I'd slip around in the mud. They don't cancel soccer practice because of rain.

For breakfast this morning, got out Eva's *Recipes for Success on the Field* cookbook and made health shake with brewer's yeast, protein powder, tofu, lecithin, and raw peanuts.
  UGH!!
  Meditated to improve soccer performance. Sickening taste in mouth prevented concentration.

Jogged three times around block by self.

Ate two ice cream sandwiches to get rid of health shake aftertaste.

Kicked soccer ball up porch steps. Fifty-one kicks. Hole in screen door a little bigger. (No one has noticed yet.)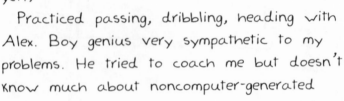

Practiced passing, dribbling, heading with Alex. Boy genius very sympathetic to my problems. He tried to coach me but doesn't know much about noncomputer-generated soccer.

Managed to conceal what I am doing from twin SuperSibs. SuperSister Eva went to swim at the high school pool. SuperSister Isabel made an emergency shopping trip to the mall for nail polish. She is obsessed by fingernails. Maybe they're her good luck charm.

Nothing will stop Abby Hayes!!!

Later on Sunday
Went to park after lunch. New girl, Natalie, was sitting under a tree reading Harry Potter book. (Question: Does she

shower with Harry Potter book?)
Told me that her parents made
her go to the park. Reason:
She needs exercise and fresh
air. She sneaked book out
under her sweatshirt.

Asked her if she would like
to practice soccer with me. She said yes,
this way she wouldn't lie to her parents
when they asked her if she got some
exercise.

We kicked the ball around for a while. I
am better at soccer than Natalie. She is
not crazy about sports. Says she
prefers to read, solve mysteries,
and do chemistry experiments. Once
she made a powder in her chemistry lab that turned her hands
blue for a week. I said that
maybe I should get some for Isabel. Then
her hands would match her fingernails!

I asked Natalie how she liked our
school. She said it is much better than her
old school. At her old school, there were
thirty-five kids in each class instead of

twenty-two. They only had music once a week instead of twice a week, and they didn't have creative writing! She likes Ms. Bunder, too.

Before we went home, Natalie said she was glad her parents made her go to the park.

Definitely like Natalie. She could be new friend.

Hayes Family News
Heard at Dinner Table

At Sunday night dinner, the Hayes family shared their news for the week.

Olivia Hayes has received a promotion to full partner in her law firm.

Paul Hayes has landed a new and important account.

Between large forkfuls of mashed potatoes, Eva Hayes mentioned that she broke the school record for freestyle swimming. She has also been elected captain of her basketball and lacrosse teams.

Her high school teachers have nominated Isabel Hayes (Lady of the Perfect Fingernails) to represent our city in a nationwide History Contest. She will go to Washington, D.C., in the spring.

Alex Hayes is designing his own computer game, which he plans to market and sell on the Web. He will probably be a millionaire by the time he's nine.

As for Abby Hayes, she had nothing to say.

Must become top soccer player. Must, must, must!

Studied Sunday sports page after dinner. Inspiring story of athlete who overcame cancer to win race. I have so much less to overcome. Must not give up. Must redouble my efforts. Note: Why don't people say "retriple" efforts? That is more like it. I must retriple my efforts.

More health shakes!
More sit-ups!
More soccer practices!

Soccer Tip of the Day: Practice using

both feet, so you can kick the ball no matter what angle it comes at you from.

If fight with best friend continues, will have lunch with Natalie tomorrow in school. Wonder if Natalie can concoct a sports powder in her chemistry lab that will make me a soccer star. Wonder if she can make a friendship powder to reunite fighting friends.

This is the last thing I'll write for today! Promise!
Really, I mean it. Help! I can't stop writing. I can't stop . . . Can't stop. . . . I am haunted by the Spirit of the Pen. Bye for now!!!!

Chapter 7

> Monday
>
> "If at first you don't succeed, try, try again."
> (Until you get exhausted.)
>
> **World Cup Soccer Calendar**

Push-ups: twelve. Sit-ups: nine. Collapsed sneezing on floor because of dust in carpet. It's Isabel's week to vacuum. She doesn't do *everything* perfectly!

Made power shake of protein powder, dried fruits, milk powder, protein enzymes, pineapple juice, vitamin C drink, lecithin, and raisins.

Forced self to drink almost all of it. Poured rest down sink. Foamed going down the drain. Is this cause for alarm or sign that it is already working?

Read sports page. Woman who was ranked last in marathon became first through hard work, determination, and belief in herself. This could happen to me.

Jogged around block five times with backpack for weight training. Schoolbooks squished lunch. Strawberry jelly on homework. Wiped it off. Made new sandwich. Used powerful self-discipline and did not lick jelly from fingers.

Joke of the day: Why do soccer players never get hot?

Answer: Because of all their fans.

Good news of the day!

Jessica came over before school and apologized. She said she invited Eva to play soccer because she was mad at me for lying. She said she was sorry she had done it.

I apologized for quitting the game. I said that next time I had to fib to my sisters, I wouldn't use her as an excuse.

"Why can't you tell them the truth?" she asked.

"I try to, but sometimes I can't! How would you feel if you had twin sisters who were better than you at EVERY-THING? And they let you know it!"

Jessica thought about it. "It would drive me crazy," she finally said.

She has no siblings (lucky!) and only one parent, who is definitely not perfect!

Then we both apologized and cried and hugged and promised never to fight again. Hooray! It is wonderful to have a best friend!

I told her about meeting Natalie in the park and said that maybe we could all get together after school. She thought that was a good idea.

"Ssst!" Abby pointed to Tyler's open knapsack and the Game Boy that was peeking out of it. She remembered that Ms. Kantor had announced that she would "confiscate all games and game stations" if she found them in school.

Tyler looked at her blankly.

"Your Game Boy!" Abby said.

"Huh?"

"Oh, forget it," Abby muttered. Why was she being so nice to Tyler, anyway? Last week in gym class he had called her "fumble foot."

Brianna had laughed loudly. Abby hoped it was because she thought Tyler was cute, not because she agreed with him.

"Put away your science projects, class." Ms. Kantor cleared her throat. "Get ready for the timed math quiz."

Several students groaned.

Ms. Kantor cleared her throat again. "I know this is everyone's least favorite activity, but it will help you at the end of the year. Clear your desks and sit quietly until everyone is ready."

Brianna sat with her hands neatly folded, a smug expression on her face.

Behind her, in an identical posture, sat Bethany.

 I wonder if Bethany takes Brianna lessons. I wonder if Tyler and Zach were born with miniature Game Boys in their hands.

Ms. Kantor began to pass out the quizzes. "Do each problem as quickly as you can. If you get stuck, go on to the next. If you have time, you can go back to it."

"Ms. Kantor! Ms. Kantor!" Brianna waved her hand. "I practiced timed tests this summer with Bethany."

"Yes, we did, Ms. Kantor," Bethany agreed.

—Brianna Brag Index: Number of times Brianna has bragged so far in class: 9 (Wait until end of day. This number may be in thousands.)

—Number of times Tyler and Zach have used the word "game" in a sentence: 1,000,000,000.

—Number of times I have written in my notebook since seven A.M.: 4

"Abby Hayes, I'm glad that you love writing so much," Ms. Kantor said. "When Ms. Bunder comes, she will be very impressed with all your writing. Now put the notebook away. We're going to begin our math quiz."

Abby slipped the notebook and her purple pen

into her desk. "Math," she muttered to herself. "Math, math, math . . ."

"We have fifteen minutes for twenty problems," Ms. Kantor announced. "I'm setting the timer now!"

Abby raced through the rows of long division and multiplication. She was a race car. She was a racehorse. She was a sprinting runner. She was . . . she was . . .

She was stuck.

What was 56.8 divided by .73, anyway? Or 85.1 times 9.13?

Math was not her best subject. It was Alex's best subject. It was Isabel's best subject (though every subject was Isabel's best).

Brianna was done already! She flounced up to Ms. Kantor to give her the completed quiz.

Then Natalie was done. Before Bethany, ha-ha-ha, Abby thought as she added a row of numbers.

Tyler and Zach were done. And Jessica, Bethany, Rachel, Meghan, Jon, Mason, Collin . . .

"Time's up!"

Abby scrawled the answer to the problem she was working on. There. She had gotten most of them finished. All but five, anyway.

"A little more focus, Abby, and you'll get them all next time," Ms. Kantor said encouragingly.

Oh, great. Something else to work on. Her brain just didn't want to focus on math these days; she had too many worries.

Becoming a soccer star was getting more and more complicated.

This morning Mr. Stevens handed out permission slips for the soccer team. They had to be signed by Thursday, the day of the first practice, and returned. Players also needed shin guards and soccer shoes.

What was she to do? How could she get her parents to sign the permission slip without telling them she was going out for the team?

Her mother, the lawyer, would not sign any paper without reading it first.

Her father was less cautious but more curious. He would want all the details. Why was she going out for the team? Who else was on it? What position did she want to play?

One of the SuperSibs would surely overhear them.

It was not easy to keep any kind of secret in the Hayes family!

If she didn't tell one of her parents, she also had to figure out who would pay for soccer cleats and shin guards. And how would she explain coming home late after practice?

Abby had to keep practicing her soccer skills, too. It was hard to tell if her program was working or not. She wondered if a month was enough time to turn herself into a soccer star.

Chapter 8

> **Thursday**
>
> "Each step is not a means to an end, but a glorious moment to be treasured for itself."
>
> Working Woman's Wisdom Calendar

No comment.

Number of colors of nail polish my sister Isabel owns: 35

Number of pairs of earrings Brianna owns: 18

Times per day Ms. Kantor says "Tyler and Zach! Pay attention!": 27 (average)

Times Tyler has picked his nose in class: 5

Number of lies I have told for soccer: 3

Number of goals I have scored: 0

Ms. Kantor is clearing her throat less now. Thank goodness! Today she is wearing a brown linen dress and white sneakers.

They are more comfortable than shoes, she says. She is nice, but Ms. Bunder is still my favorite teacher. I wish she would come every day of the week, even Saturday and Sunday.

Soccer Tip: Pass with the inside of your foot. Shoot on your shoelaces. The toe should be pointed.

Have trained for soccer all week. Drank disgusting concoctions (haven't thrown up yet, but gotten close); done sit-ups, push-ups, jumping jacks; and watched soccer games on television. Mia, Michelle, and Briana are awesome!

After watching, went up to room to meditate. Imagined self player like one on the Women's Soccer Cup Team. Heard the cheers! The crowd went wild. Felt the glory and the power. Opened eyes. Was still ordinary Abby Hayes. Looked at calendars for a while, then went into backyard to practice kicking soccer ball.

Alex came with me. He headed the ball

once! Said it made him feel dizzy.

Am still not a great athlete. Power of mind has not kicked in yet. Maybe it is like one of those slow-acting chemicals. One day, when I least expect it, I will wake up and find myself transformed.

Abby looked up. Ms. Bunder had come into the classroom while she was writing. She was wearing a red velour top with flared jeans. Her hair was braided into a bun with little red clips holding it in place.

Ms. Bunder is not only my favorite teacher, but she also wears the best clothes! Even Brianna and Bethany check out her outfits.

She is carrying a shoe box. I wonder what's inside it. Shoes? Maybe she is going to give Ms. Kantor a pair of platform sandals or some combat boots. Ha-ha.

"What's in that box?" Jessica asked.

Ms. Bunder smiled. "Our creative writing exercise for today."

"We're going to write about shoes?" Zach said.

Ms. Bunder put the box on his desk. "Take a look," she said.

Zach peered into the box and pulled out a strip of newspaper. "What's this?"

"Newspaper headlines," Ms. Bunder explained. "I've been collecting them for months."

" 'Giants on Rampage,' " Zach read. " 'Cardinals Stomp Opponents.' "

"Use the headlines to spark your imagination." Ms. Bunder picked up the box and gave it to Tyler. "Then write a poem or a story. You can use the headline for the title or the first line, if you wish. While you write, I'll take a look at your journals."

Abby picked a headline out of the shoe box, read it, and laughed out loud. "Snap Turns to Slog."

"That's one of my favorites, Abby," Ms. Bunder said. "I know you'll do something super with it."

Abby flushed with pleasure. "What did you get, Jessica?"

"Dressing Up and Down When Flying to the Sun." She made the thumbs-up sign. "Yes! Now I can write about outer space."

Natalie leaned forward to show Jessica and Abby her headline. " 'Chemical Reaction Overwhelms City.' Isn't that perfect? Now I can put in something about my chemistry experiments."

"Are you going to soccer practice after school?" Abby asked her.

"Only because my parents are making me." Natalie sighed and stared at her headline.

Jessica looked sympathetic. "We'll be there, too."

Natalie brightened up. "Great! That'll be fun!"

"Okay, everyone," Ms. Bunder said. "Get started!"

Abby picked up her pen.

I put the snap under my bed, and it turned to slog. My little brother stuck his hand into it and couldn't get it out. He was really mad because he couldn't play on his computer. When my sister tried to rescue him, she got stuck, too, and missed her basketball game. You should have heard the screams coming from my room!

At the end of the class, Ms. Bunder gathered up the stories and returned the journals. "Great job," she said to Abby as she handed hers back.

"Next week's assignment!" she announced.

"Write in your journals and read three newspaper articles. In three weeks, you'll turn in your own article. The subject can be anything you choose."

Jessica nudged Abby. "A newspaper article! That should be fun! What are you going to write about?"

"I don't know," Abby whispered back.

She was still basking in the glow of Ms. Bunder's "great" and "super." Those were the kind of comments she wanted to get about her soccer playing.

Problem: Still can't figure out difference between right offense and right defense. Why does everyone think it's so cool to hit the ball with their heads? Ouch!

The first soccer practice is today. I told my parents I was going home with Jessica after school today. It wasn't really a lie. At least not a big one. We are going to walk home together afterward. Maybe Natalie will join us.

A few hours later, Abby joined an excited group of fifth-grade girls in the gym. In her school backpack was a battered pair of shin guards she had taken from the bottom of Eva's closet. Jessica had loaned her a pair of cleats from last year that were too small for her but that fit Abby perfectly.

Mr. Stevens blew his whistle. "Has everyone turned in their permission slips?"

Abby stood quietly behind Jessica and Natalie. Maybe no one would notice she hadn't turned in a permission slip. If anyone asked her, she'd pretend she'd forgotten it or act as if she'd already given it in.

But what if Mr. Stevens knew that she hadn't? What if he called out her name and asked her to leave in front of everyone?

She should have confided in her father, Abby thought. He would have kept her secret. Now, if she were humiliated in front of Brianna, Bethany, and the rest of the fifth-grade girls, it would be her own fault. Maybe she would even get thrown off the team before it started. She might have already destroyed her chances to become a soccer star.

Jessica was right: Lying was wrong!

She crossed her fingers and knocked on wood. She promised that if she got away with it this time, she'd go right to her father after practice and ask him to sign the permission slip.

"Okay, everyone. We're going to play a practice game, then choose our captain," Mr. Stevens announced. "Our first game will be in two weeks. We'll play against other city teams. The champion will play for a county title."

"I'm going to be captain," Brianna announced, "of the champion team."

Bethany pumped her fist in the air.

"I admire your team spirit, Brianna," Mr. Stevens said. "Your teammates will choose a captain after our practice."

"I'll win." Brianna put her hands on her hips and surveyed the fifth-grade girls.

"We'll vote for you!" Rachel and Meghan said.

"A vote for Brianna is a vote for the best!" Beth-any cried. "Yay, Brianna!"

Jessica nudged Abby. "Nominate me," she said.

"You?"

She nodded.

"Okay." Abby was surprised. She didn't know that Jessica wanted to be captain. But one thing was for sure: If she won, she'd be a big improvement over Brianna.

The fifth-graders put on blue-and-yellow pinneys. Then they trooped outside to the soccer field to play.

Chapter 9

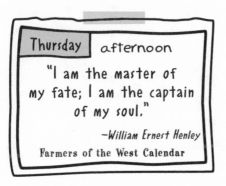

Thursday afternoon

"I am the master of my fate; I am the captain of my soul."

—William Ernest Henley

Farmers of the West Calendar

But who will be the captain of my soccer team? Soccer Tip: Do NOT look down. Do NOT watch ball. Otherwise you will not see where you're going.

"Pass the ball, Abby!" Bethany cried. "Over here!"

The ball was coming straight toward her. It seemed to be moving in slow motion. Abby took a deep breath and prepared to intercept it.

Now was her chance to prove herself in the very first practice. So far, she hadn't done much to help her side. On the other hand, she hadn't done anything awful, either.

The ball was coming closer. What should she do? Dribble it, juggle it, head it? When it came to soccer, she was like a baby who knew how to talk but not to walk.

Suddenly, as if through its own will, her foot shot out and connected solidly with the ball.

"That's it!" Jessica yelled. "Go, Abby!"

Her foot had done the job, Abby told herself in awe. A mysterious instinct had taken over. Her body had known what to do. Maybe she did have a hidden talent!

The ball zoomed past Natalie, who tried feebly to kick it.

Then Brianna ran toward it, but Rachel from the other side had already intercepted it. She kicked it straight into the goal.

"Point!" Mr. Stevens yelled.

Her teammates rushed to hug Rachel.

Brianna glared at Natalie. "That's your fault!" she hissed. Natalie shrugged and walked away.

"You'll do better next time," Abby consoled her.

She was still aglow with her success of a moment ago. Even though the other side had made the point, her pass was still a miracle, a breakthrough, an amazing moment of grace for Abby. It was a sign that she was on her way.

Mr. Stevens smiled at her. "Keep up the great work, Abby. Practice, practice, practice."

The whole world was going to love her when she became a soccer star. She imagined her family beaming at her; her teammates congratulating her; Ms. Bunder saying, "I knew you could do it." Even Brianna would have to admit that Abby was a star when she scored point after point for the team.

Mr. Stevens clapped his hands for the game to resume.

Abby ran up and down the field, chasing the ball, hoping for another chance to make a pass. But the ball didn't come her way again, or else she wasn't fast enough to intercept it.

At the end of the practice, the two sides were tied. Hot, sweaty, and tired, the girls gathered in a circle to vote for a captain.

"I nominate Brianna," Bethany cried. "She's the best! B for Brianna and best!"

"Any other nominations?" Mr. Stevens asked.

Abby jumped to her feet. "I nominate Jessica! She's fair and fun."

"Anyone else?"

No one spoke up.

"Okay, let's take a vote. Everyone for Brianna, raise your hand."

Mr. Stevens counted. "It's going to be close. Now for Jessica."

He counted again. "Brianna is the winner by five votes."

"Yay, Brianna!" yelled Bethany, jumping up and down like a cheerleader.

"Sorry," Abby said to Jessica. "You would have been a good captain."

"It's okay." Jessica shrugged. "I got more votes than I expected."

Brianna stood up. "We are going to win, win, win!" she cried. "Only the best will play on our team! Who's the best?"

"We are!" The girls roared back.

"We're number one! We're number one! We're the winning team! Only the best will play! B-E-S-T!" she spelled, as if they were all kindergartners.

Abby caught Jessica's eye.

She knew her best friend didn't care that she had lost the vote to be captain. But she still wished Jessica had won.

Not only would Jessica have been a kinder, gentler captain, but she would have helped and encouraged Abby more on her way to becoming a soccer star. Today was a great start — but it was only the beginning. There was a lot of work ahead of her, more than she ever would have believed.

Chapter 10

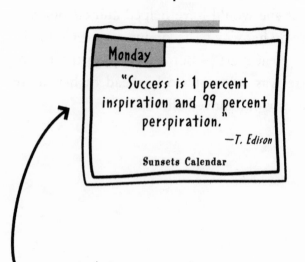

Monday

"Success is 1 percent inspiration and 99 percent perspiration."
—T. Edison

Sunsets Calendar

as quoted by my mother, who never perspires.

I am perspiring a lot! So I should be a success at soccer. Right?

I've only had one moment of inspiration! It wasn't 1 percent — more like .0001 percent.

So where do you get the inspiration? In your sleep? While arguing with siblings? With a butterfly net?

Abby's Soccer Goal Progress

Drank power health shake with protein powder, soy milk granules, brewer's yeast, energy formula, tofu, lecithin, and a few marshmallows thrown in for taste.

Double UGH!

Meditated. Did not let mind become distracted by terrible taste in mouth and sickening sensation in stomach. Focused on feet and knees. Imagined them connecting with ball again and again.

Leg lifts. Back twists. Abdominal crunches.

Reviewed World Cup game on VCR.

Practiced with Jessica. Juggled ball twice. Kicked it lots of times. Kicked self only once. Big improvement.

New friend, Natalie, joined in. She said I was getting better, too.

After our practice, decided it was time to tell my father the truth about soccer.

Number of times I cleared my throat before telling him: 12.

Number of deep breaths I took: so many that he thought I was doing yoga exercises.

Times I made him promise never, ever to

tell my SuperSisters: 16.

Kisses he got after he said, "Don't worry; your secret is safe with me. Now give me that permission slip to sign! You have to turn one in, especially with a lawyer for a mother." I gave him at least 100 kisses! And he hadn't shaved, either.

What my father said: "If anyone asks where you are, Abby, I'll say you're with Jessica. I just won't mention that you're playing soccer. You have the right to keep a harmless secret from your sisters."

Tomorrow we have another timed math quiz coming up. (GROAN) I *hate* timed math quizzes! They are hard! I hate fractions! I hate decimals! And I hate multiplying and dividing them!

In other late-breaking news, we had soccer practice after school today. I felt good turning in my permission slip to Mr. Stevens. He made me goalie for the first part of the game. You have to wear a cage on your face and layers of padding on your stomach and chest. I felt like an alien bumblebee!

The goalie is the only person in the game who can throw the ball with her hands.

<u>Soccer Tip for Goalies</u>

Don't try to catch the ball. Block it with your hands instead!

Brianna got really mad after the other side scored three points in a row, and demanded to put another goalie in.

If she gets this upset about a practice, what will she be like at the game?

Must rid self of habit of flinching when soccer ball comes near upper body. Try to head it instead.

The soccer game will be on television in half an hour. Must study math in meantime. Do not want to study math. Prefer to have injection of second-grade brother's brain cells instead.

Must study soccer. Must continue to watch great soccer players and then visualize self doing same moves.

Read in book that way to success is to write goals one hundred times a day. If this is what it takes, I will do it. Get ready, set, GO!

I will become a soccer star by the end of soccer season.

I will become a soccer star by the end of soccer season.

I will become a soccer star by the end of soccer season.

I will become a soccer star by the end of soccer season.

I will become a soccer star by the end of socc . . . . .

In this family, there are too many interruptions! Just a minute ago, Isabel barged into my room.

"Where is my nail polish?" she demanded. "Have you seen my nail polish?"

How does she have time to be a top student and president of her class and still spend every spare moment thinking about nail polish?

I held up my pale, unvarnished nails. "The evidence says I am NOT guilty."

She flew out of my room, not wasting precious seconds on apologies.

"Eva!" she shrieked. "Eva!"

If she had asked me, I would have told her not to bother. Eva doesn't care about nail polish. Alex is the guilty culprit. He is probably building a supercomputer out of microchips, old wires, and nail polish that can do all of our homework and take out the garbage, too. I wouldn't put it past him.

I will become a soccer star by the end of soccer season.

I will become a soccer star by the end of soccer season.

I will become a soccer star by the end

of soccer season.

I will . . .

This is boring! Do I have to do it all at once? Maybe I can finish later.

Need to think of newspaper article idea for Ms. Bunder's class, anyway. (Will study math in morning.)

Title of Brianna's interview with herself: "My Life As Soccer Captain"

Title of my imaginary interview with Brianna: "Bragging Brianna Bores All"

Actual title of Zach's newspaper article: "Electronic Games"

Actual title of Tyler's newspaper article: "Electronic Games"

(Wow. Exciting.)

Title of Jessica's article: "Intelligent Life in the Universe: True or False?"

Title of my article:

I don't have a single idea yet! Lucky it's not due for a while.

I will become a soccer star by the end of soccer season.

I will become a soccer star by the end of soccer season.

I will definitely and without a shadow of a doubt become a soccer star by the end . . .

Yelling outside my door. The SuperSibs are having a "friendly discussion." Sounds more like World War III. I better stop now before they burst into my . . . Uh-oh, here they come!!!

G O O D - B Y E . . .

Chapter 11

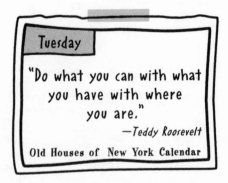

Tuesday

"Do what you can with what
you have with where
you are."
—*Teddy Roosevelt*
Old Houses of New York Calendar

What I did: Flunked math test.

What I have to do: Take it over.

Where I will be if my parents learn about it: Grounded.

Ms. Kantor was VERY nice! She said, "This isn't like you, Abby. I know you're trying hard. Everyone has a bad day now and then. Study some more and you can make it up tomorrow."

Felt ashamed. The truth is I didn't study this morning like I planned.

Instead stood on head to make blood

flow to brain. (It didn't work.)
Also made super power health
formula drink. Put in dried chestnut
powder, bean flour, nonfat dried
milk granules, wheat germ, protein
formula, yeast, a few soy beans,
carob powder, and some banana
chips for taste.

Do athletes *really* drink this stuff?? *No*
wonder they're always exercising! They have
to distract themselves from the revolting
taste!

Found five biographies of famous athletes
in Eva's room. Started first after breakfast.

Ms. Kantor almost as wonderful as Ms.
Bunder. (It's not her fault that I like
creative writing better than any other
subject.)

Will study fractions and decimals tonight
— *promise!*

Chapter 12

Thursday

"Every cloud has a silver lining."

The Big Sky Calendar

Have you ever seen a silver lining in a cloud? No! I haven't, either. Clouds are white puffy things. Sometimes the sun makes them look reddish or gold, but NEVER silver. Who came up with this stupid saying, anyway? It's completely false!

Passed math test — just barely. Ms. Kantor says I need extra help. She is going to put me in the math tutorial group.
It's true! I need help! Though not the way she thinks.

What Should Have Happened
at the First Soccer Game

Abby Hayes made use of all the soccer
tips she studied and practiced so hard. Her
teamwork with Jessica and Natalie was
especially brilliant. With stunning precision,
the fifth-grader, who began playing soccer
only a few short weeks ago, scored all of
the goals in the first, second, and third
periods, leading her team to victory. For once
in her life, Brianna was speechless. Not a
brag came out of her mouth.

"Yay, Abby!" Bethany cheered.

Mr. Stevens told Abby that she must
continue drinking her power health formulas
because he was going to put her in every
single game for the rest of the season.

What Could Have Happened

Abby Hayes continued to improve her
soccer game. While not the star player,
she made some solid passes, enabling her
teammates to score goals. She prevented the
other team from scoring on several occasions,
and even headed the ball once.

What Really Happened

I don't want to talk about it.

Aftergame Comments

"Why don't you bring a good book to the next game? And a pillow, in case you get tired. Be sure to rest if you need to." Brianna, concerned about my health.

"Nice job, Abby. Fine effort. Keep up the good work." Mr. Stevens would say this to a corpse.

"You're getting better, Abby. Don't worry; ups and downs are part of the game." Best friend, Jessica, always has something positive to say. (She had asthma attack in middle of second period and had to sit out.)

"It's just a game. I'm only here because my parents are making me. Who cares whether you're a star or not? I like you the way you are." New friend Natalie's kind words did not make me feel better.

Terrible, awful game. Missed every pass.

Let other team score winning point.

Hope gone. Cloud very dark and covering entire sky. No little beam of sunshine. Good resolutions broken. Power of mind squashed. Inspiring words useless.

Chapter 13

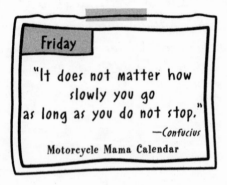

Friday

"It does not matter how
slowly you go
as long as you do not stop."
—Confucius
Motorcycle Mama Calendar

I read these inspiring words this morning, and they did not inspire me. They depressed me.

What if I don't want to go on and on forever at a slow pace? What if I want to spurt ahead? Or *nothing*?

Lay in bed this morning until Dad got me up.

Did not have heart to make power health drink. Made strawberry milk shake instead.

Recipe: two scoops strawberry ice cream, one scoop vanilla ice cream, milk, and some vanilla extract. Throw in blender and drink as fast as you can before parents or twin siblings see what you are having for breakfast. Offer some to sympathetic younger brother who promises he won't tell on you.

Returned famous athletes' biographies to Eva's room. Read comics with Alex at breakfast table.

Completed all homework.

"I wonder if Quidditch is as difficult as soccer." Natalie sighed and took a bite from a chocolate bar. "Harry Potter seems to enjoy it more."

"I'd rather be flying than fouling," Abby agreed.

"Soccer's not that bad," Jessica said. "It's even fun once you get the hang of it." She took a puff from her inhaler.

"Are you okay?" Abby was worried about Jessica. Her asthma seemed to be worse lately.

"The fall is hard," Jessica said, wheezing a little. "It's all the pollen in the air. After the first frost, things get better. I'll be all right."

"You still manage to score a lot of points in soc-cer," Abby said. "You do a lot better than me."

The three girls sat on a bench in the park, their

backpacks at their feet. Across from them, a group of preschoolers watched ducks swim in the pond.

"I'm not making much progress." Abby took a deep breath and spoke the words she had been thinking since last night. "Maybe I should quit soccer now before I make a complete fool of myself."

Thinking about it made her feel shaky, as if she were about to leap off a cliff without a parachute. Would she be letting her father down? Would she be letting her team down? Would she be letting herself down after all the work and effort she had put in?

Jessica came swiftly to her defense. "That's not true! You've improved a lot."

"Yes, I've scored fewer points for the other team lately."

"Someone has to help them along," Jessica joked.

Abby ran her hands through her hair. It felt even wilder and redder and more out of control than usual.

"You're more confident than you used to be," her best friend pointed out.

"I'm making more mistakes," Abby said.

"You've got way more courage and determination."

"Really?" Maybe Jessica meant that she took more

foolhardy risks, like getting in the way of the ball when it was speeding toward her. "I don't think so."

"Yes," Natalie and Jessica said in unison. "You do."

Had she really transformed herself into a confident, brave, and determined fifth-grader?

If so, it could mean only one thing: The inspiring words and slogans that Abby had pumped into her mind like multivitamins had worked.

She had built up her mental muscle to such a degree that it was only a matter of time before she became a top soccer player. If faith could move mountains, it could surely kick a few soccer balls.

"There's hope!" she cried.

Or was there?

Was she deceiving herself, thinking she could become a great soccer player?

Natalie took another bite from her chocolate bar. "I wish I wanted to be a good soccer player. All I want to do is sit in my room and read or perform experiments. My parents think I'm warped."

"Really? My parents would love you," Abby said. "They think Isabel is great, and she spends her entire life in the library. Except when she's doing her fingernails, of course."

"Wow," Natalie said. "Awesome."

Yes, Abby's family was awesome. That was the problem. She picked up her journal.

If family is awesome, then I must be, too. Genetic heritage must show up somewhere. Even if they are type A and I am type Z. Curly red hair and lack of genius are not proof that I come from different genetic line. Amazing gene must be hiding, but one day it will show up.

Right?

If A gene doesn't show up soon, will replace World Cup Soccer calendar with School Joke calendar.

Burning question of the day: What to do about soccer goals. Can I achieve them? How soon? Soon enough to make a difference and impress my family?

Do I hope for the best and continue? Or cut my losses and quit?

Note: Why are questions burning? Can they be cold? Or soothing?

Why are losses cut? Why not sliced? Or chopped?

Must not be distracted by these deep thoughts. Back to my friends and the decision I must make.

Abby put down her pen. Her two friends were looking over their journals. Jessica had doodled pictures of aliens in the margins of hers; Natalie had written only a few paragraphs in large letters.

"I wish I loved to write as much as you, Abby." Natalie sighed. "I don't know what I'm going to do about this newspaper article."

"Neither do I," Abby admitted. "But I'll probably get an idea sooner or later." She took the piece of chocolate that Natalie held out to her. "Why don't you write a book review of the Harry Potter series?"

Natalie's face brightened. "Good idea!"

"When I get stuck writing a story, I always ask Abby for help," Jessica said.

"It's fun," Abby said. "I love to do it." She wished that soccer came as easily as writing.

"So . . . what do you think?" Jessica asked. "About soccer. Are you going to quit or not?"

"I vote for Abby to stay with it!" Natalie cried. "I think she can do it."

"You never know what you can do until you try," Jessica said, pulling out her asthma inhaler and taking another puff.

Was this a sign? Her best friend was spouting inspiring slogans just like one of Abby's calendars. Maybe it meant that Abby wasn't supposed to give up.

Jessica had asthma, but she didn't let it stop her. Abby didn't have asthma, and she was ready to quit.

Natalie was rooting for her, too. She couldn't disappoint her friends.

She hoped she wouldn't disappoint herself.

"Okay. I won't quit yet," Abby announced. "I'll stay in until the end of soccer season."

Chapter 14

Saturday

"Hope is a waking dream."
—*Aristotle*

Spuds Calendar

(Aristotle again. Isabel says that he lived in ancient Greece. Wonder if he collected calendars, too.) It's easy to hope on the weekend when there aren't any games. What I really hope for is an idea for that newspaper article. It's due this week. I've been so busy thinking about soccer that I haven't done anything about the article at all! I can't fail math and creative writing! (Especially since creative writing is my best subject.)

This morning: Made another power health

shake: vitamin-enriched brewer's yeast, non-fat yogurt, soy flakes, dried apple rings, grapefruit juice, protein powder, oat bran.

Ugh! Ugh! UGH!

Wrote "I will become a star soccer player . . ." 150 times on piece of paper. Hung it on wall next to World Soccer Cup calendar.

Exercises: Deep breathing, sit-ups, push-ups, jumping jacks, leg lifts, shoulder rolls, neck rolls, dinner rolls (ha-ha, just kidding).

Stood on head to make blood flow to brain. Power health shake flowed from stomach to mouth. Ugh!

Took biographies of great athletes out of Eva's room again and read for half an hour. Eva didn't notice.

Called Jessica and asked her to meet me in park later this afternoon for more soccer practice. Natalie is in middle of important experiment and can't come.

"Hey, Abby. What's up?" It was Eva, in

her customary outfit of basketball jersey and shorts, dribbling a basketball on the sidewalk in front of Abby.

"Trying to come up with an idea for an article. For creative writing class." Abby sighed. She had been staring at the blank paper for twenty minutes now. Her mind was crammed with soccer tips, inspiring stories about athletes who had come up from under, and flashbacks to exciting moments on the soccer field. There was no room in her brain for anything else.

Abby didn't know if Ms. Bunder would be as understanding as Ms. Kantor if she turned in her article late. Maybe she would even give Abby a failing grade!

Eva whirled and feigned a shot. Then she turned back to Abby. "You're always writing," she said. "A newspaper article should be easy for you."

"It isn't this time," Abby admitted.

"Why don't you cover one of my basketball games?"

"I don't know enough about the rules and who the players are."

"I'd fill you in," Eva offered. "You can publish it in your school newspaper, too."

"We don't have one," Abby said.

"Maybe you should start one," Eva said, wiping her forehead with the back of her hand.

"Maybe . . ." Abby echoed. It was a good idea. After soccer season was over, she'd talk to Ms. Bunder and see if Natalie and Jessica were interested.

That still left her without a subject for her article.

Or did it?

She couldn't cover Eva's basketball game — there was too much to learn first. However, there was another game where she knew both the players and the rules. She had spent plenty of time observing the action. In addition, she had firsthand, personal experience. If Abby wasn't qualified to write about the Lancaster Elementary fifth-grade girls' soccer team, who was?

Hadn't she been obsessed with soccer for weeks? Here was the article idea, practically begging to be written, and she hadn't even thought of it until Eva made her suggestion.

She jumped up from the steps and hugged her sister. "Thanks, Eva. You're the greatest."

Eva smiled. Everyone always told her she was the greatest. She didn't even ask Abby why.

"You should wear your hair down more often,"

she said, looking at Abby's long curly red hair.

"You like my hair?" Abby couldn't believe it. "It's so red! It's so messy and tangly!"

"It's so gorgeous," Eva said. "If you were stuck with boring straight brown hair like me, you'd appreciate it. I've been jealous of your hair since you were a baby."

"You have?"

"Whenever you get sick of it, give it to me." Eva dropped the basketball into a bin on the porch and disappeared into the house to take a shower.

Abby stared openmouthed after her sister. This was Eva, wasn't it? Not some alien inhabiting her sister's body?

Wow. SuperSib Eva, family jock, gave me an idea for the newspaper article AND she loves my hair!!!! Stunning surprise. SuperSis can behave differently than expected. Maybe I can, too. Stay tuned for further developments.

Abby pulled a fresh sheet of paper from her notebook and began to work on her article.

Chapter 15

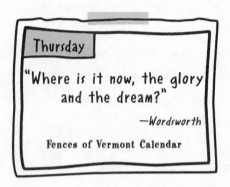

Thursday

"Where is it now, the glory
and the dream?"

—Wordsworth

Fences of Vermont Calendar

Alive, well, and kicking. It's my lucky
week – and there's a game tonight.

<u>Lucky Week List</u>

#1. I completed the newspaper article and
turned it in on time!

Didn't have to make embarrassing
explanations or apologies to Ms. Bunder. I
wouldn't want her to think I don't care
about creative writing class. Because it is
my FAVORITE subject in the world!

Ms. Bunder smiled when she saw the title and said she couldn't wait to read it.

#2. I got an 85 percent on a timed math quiz!!! (How did I do that? It really was luck.)

Ms. Kantor wrote, "Keep up the good work!" and gave me a pizza certificate for my effort.

Zach said he'd rather have a computer game.

I said, "If they gave out computer games as rewards, you'd be the best student in the school."

Zach agreed. Then he said, "But no one would be better than you in writing."

Agree with Brianna for once. Zach is cute. (When not hooked up to a game machine. Then he is like an electronic zombie.)

#3. Today Brianna is not in school!!!

Bethany told us that Brianna spent last

night throwing up and is still sick today. How many times did she puke? Could start Brianna Barf Index instead of Brianna Brag Index.

Mr. Stevens says that Jessica will be the temporary captain for the soccer game tonight. She will assign positions. Hooray!

Bethany is sulking because Jessica is captain. She thought she should be captain because she is best friend and best clone of Brianna.

"It's not a look-alike contest," I told her. "Almost half the players voted for Jessica."

Personally, I am very happy that Bethany will not lead our team to misery. Many of the other players seem pleased about it, too.

A lot of people are coming to today's game. Ms. Kantor is coming because we are playing Swiss Hill Elementary, her old school. She says she will root for us and not them.

Jessica's mother is taking off early from

work to see the game—and she doesn't even know that Jessica will be captain!

Natalie is glad that her parents can't come. They have already threatened to make her play basketball, softball, and lacrosse. If they see how bad she is, she says, they might make her take up volleyball and cross-country skiing as well.

Jessica's asthma is worse today, and she had to go to the nurse's office twice to use her inhaler. She is also nervous about the game.

She said she is worried about all the people who will be watching. Her mother isn't able to come to many of her games. Jessica wants her mother to see her at her best.

I told her, "You never know what you can do until you try," and "We must cultivate our garden."

Jessica said she didn't know what gardens had to do with it, but she was glad that I was her friend. She said she would try to enjoy the game and not worry so much about what everyone was thinking.

Have not given up hope of becoming soccer star. Sign of insanity? There is none in immediate family.

It's my lucky week. Anything can happen!

Encouraging, positive attitude of best friend and temporary soccer captain will no doubt make me a better player."

The Lancaster girls put on their shin guards and cleats and kicked the ball back and forth on the field to warm up.

The Swiss Hill team arrived.

"Okay, let's go out and have fun!" Jessica yelled.

"Brianna would never say 'fun,' " Bethany pouted. "She'd say win! Let's go out and win!!"

"If we don't win, we can still have fun!" Jessica retorted.

The team cheered. "Hooray, Lancaster Elementary!"

They ran onto the field and took up their positions.

The ball went into play. Jessica passed it to

Bethany. Bethany kicked it to Rachel, who dribbled it toward the goal until a girl on the other team stole it from her.

Abby ran after the Swiss Hill girl. She came up alongside her, kicked the ball out from under her, and raced in the opposite direction for the goal.

"Abby! Abby! Abby!" shrieked her teammates.

She barely heard them as she weaved in and out of the Swiss Hill guards, keeping the ball under control. The field seemed to open up as she ran. It was as though a path were marked straight to the goal.

Ms. Kantor cheered from the bleachers, and the team went wild as Abby gave the ball a ferocious kick. It soared straight into the goal, past the goalie.

"Point to Lancaster Elementary!" the ref called.

Abby pushed her damp hair off her forehead and stared at the ball in awe. She had really done it; she had scored a point for her team.

Jessica hugged Abby. "I knew you could do it!" Her teammates gave her the thumbs-up sign as she jogged back to her position.

A Swiss Hill girl stood on the midfield line and kicked the ball to one of her teammates. The game was on again.

This was the breakthrough, Abby thought. Her moment had come. When the ball soared through the air in her direction, she headed it. It bounced toward Rachel, who passed it to Jessica. Jessica raced with it toward the goal. Another point for Lancaster Elementary!

Bethany made another point, and Meghan made another. When the period ended, Lancaster was ahead.

"I knew this would happen," Abby said to Jessica, who nodded her head in agreement.

It had finally paid off. The soccer games she had watched on television, the power health formulas she had forced herself to drink, the books she had read, the inspiring words, and most of all, the hours she had practiced were leading her toward soccer stardom.

Someday, her friends would tell the story of how she had overcome incredible odds to achieve her soccer goals. For today, Abby was going to enjoy her rapid ascent to the top.

Jessica's mother was sitting on the bleachers, still in her work clothes. She had come directly from the music library at the university where she worked.

Abby waved to her, and she waved back. She only

wished that her own family was waving proudly from the bleachers. Two brilliant moves in only a matter of minutes!

Mr. Stevens blew his whistle, and they were back on the field for the second period.

Once more Abby raced for the ball. She passed it to Meghan.

"Keep it up, Abby!" Mr. Stevens yelled. "Stay in there!"

Swiss Hill intercepted the ball. Bethany stole it from the Swiss Hill girl and passed it to Abby.

"Center! Center!" Bethany screamed. "Get it, Abby!"

Abby began to sprint toward the ball. She was just about to deliver another powerful kick that would cement her reputation as a top player when she hit a patch of muddy grass. The ball whizzed past her. She slipped, lost her balance, and flew with arms outspread, facedown into the mud.

Her teammates screamed. The Swiss Hill girls cheered. Someone kicked the ball into a goal. The ref blew his whistle and declared a point for Swiss Hill.

Mr. Stevens ran over to Abby and helped her up. "That was quite an impressive fall," he said. "Anything broken?"

"I don't think so." She was covered in mud. Her T-shirt hung from her chest. Her shin guards were soaked. Her knees were scraped, and her hands were sore.

He examined her bruises. "Maybe you better sit down. We'll clean up your hands and knees and give you an ice pack."

She stumbled over to the bench where a couple of the girls were sitting out the period. Mr. Stevens sent one of them in to replace her.

"Are you all right?" Natalie asked. "You were great just a minute ago. I was cheering for you!"

"I'm okay," Abby said, her eyes filling with tears in spite of herself. The game had started so well! Now her hands and knees were stinging, and she had the taste of mud in her mouth.

Ms. Kantor climbed down the bleachers. "Your dad and brother are here, Abby."

"My dad and brother?"

Abby turned. Alex and her father were right behind her. They had come to her game!

"When did you get here?" she stammered.

"Just before you fell," her father said. "Are you okay? That was some tumble."

"Abby! You look like a mud monster!" Alex cried.

Abby stared at them in horror. She tried to say something, but no words came out.

"Your mother wants to talk to you." Her father held out a cell phone. "I told her about your fall —"

"Mom . . ." Abby said. "Yes, I'm okay." She wasn't about to tell her mother that she had tried to prove herself worthy of the Hayes family and failed. Her pity would be worse than any scorn. She handed the phone back to her father.

"What's the matter?" he asked. "We're proud of you, Abby."

Proud? For falling on her face in front of her friends, teacher, and family? She didn't think so. Abby turned and ran.

Ignoring her bruised knee, scraped palms, and the tears running down her face, she didn't stop until she reached her house. She grabbed the key from its hiding place, unlocked the door, and went straight to the bathroom. She stripped off her wet and muddy clothes and jumped into the shower. Before anyone returned, she was in her room and under the covers.

There she stayed for the rest of the night.

Chapter 16

Nothing. No words at all, especially so-called inspiring ones. Didn't they get me into this mess in the first place?

The sun streamed into Abby's bedroom. As she did every morning, she opened her eyes to walls of calendars. There was her Cats of Rhode Island calendar, featuring an orange-striped tabby for the month of October. She gazed fondly at a photograph of mashed potatoes from her Spuds calendar, then moved over to her World Soccer Cup calendar.

Abby closed her eyes and groaned as memories of the previous day flooded back.

Her parents, twin sisters, and little brother had come to her door last night. They tried to talk to her, but she refused to speak. She lay under the covers with her hands over her ears and her eyes shut tight.

More from habit than anything else, she reached over to the night table for her journal.

Cannot face family after humilation of yesterday. Triumph unseen. Spectacular nosedive into mud witnessed by entire world. (Well, almost.)

Do not want to see anyone ever again.

Options:

Spend rest of life in bed.

Get adopted by other family in other city.

Run away and live in sewers.

Tears trickled down the side of her nose as she thought of herself clothed in ragged bell-bottom jeans and a ripped tie-dye T, hunting for rats to eat for dinner.

Perhaps my wounds are so serious I will have to spend a month in the hospital recuperating. When I come out, no one will remember me.

Abby rolled back the covers and examined her knee. It was scraped and red. There wasn't any scab. Her hands didn't have a mark on them.

She lay back on the bed and tried to look pale and sickly. "My stomach hurts," she whimpered. "My head hurts. I must have gotten mud poisoning. Call the ambulance."

Someone was running up the stairs. Abby closed her eyes and lay limp on the bed. The door opened.

"Abby! Abby! Wake up!" It was Alex. He shook her gently.

She snored a little and rolled over.

He shook her harder. "Wake up!"

If she didn't open her eyes, he'd give up eventually. She just wouldn't move until he left.

Abby lay still, pretending she was dead. Alex was here to mourn her.

So why did he keep bumping against the bed and laughing?

"Wake up, Abby!" Alex said. "You're famous!"

Infamous was probably more like it. She was a laughingstock at Lancaster Elementary and in the amazing, awesome Hayes family.

Her parents' voices floated down the hall. Now they were in her room, too. Why didn't everyone just bring their bowls and plates and eat breakfast on her bed?

"Abby, the Journal has printed your newspaper article," her father announced. "Your entire family is extremely proud of you."

"What article?" She sat bolt upright and snatched the newspaper from his outstretched hand.

"I knew she wasn't sleeping!" Alex crowed.

Abby scanned the page, then saw the headline. "It's a Kick — Or Is It? The Ups and Downs of Soccer" by Abby Hayes.

"That's the article I wrote for creative writing!" Abby cried. "I just turned it in! How did it get in the paper?"

"Ms. Bunder liked your article so much that she showed it to a friend who works at the newspaper. Last night she called to let us know that it was going into print," her mother said.

Her father beamed at her. "You're a published journalist at age ten!"

"Hooray, Abby!" Alex cheered. He jumped on the bed to hug her. Her parents kissed her.

Abby's mother checked her watch. "Oops! I have to leave in fifteen minutes. Abby, get dressed and come downstairs. Your father is making waffles to celebrate."

Abby sat at the table and gazed proudly at her newspaper article. There it was, her name in print! The Journal had written an introduction: "We are pleased to present the original and thoughtful views of Abby Hayes, a fifth-grade writing student of Ms. Elizabeth Bunder at Lancaster Elementary School."

"The original and thoughtful views," Abby said out loud. "The original and thoughtful views of Abby Hayes, fifth-grade writing student."

She took a bite of waffle, which she had smeared with strawberry jam.

Then she gazed at the article again.

It's a Kick — Or Is It?
The Ups and Downs of Soccer
by Abby Hayes

Have you ever seen a team of fifth-grade girls racing

up and down a soccer field, chasing a little white ball? It's not an unusual sight at Lancaster Elementary School, where the team meets once a week to practice soccer and once a week to play in a game against another city team. The captain is Brianna Bauer. She thinks winning is important. Mr. Stevens, the coach, talks about good sportsmanship and doing your best.

Many of the girls have already been playing soccer for several years. Their heroes are Mia Hamm, Michelle Akers and Briana Scurry. They watch the World Cup on television and practice kicking soccer balls the way most kids eat candy. Some of the girls, however, are newcomers to the game. When they see a fast-moving ball coming straight at their head, they duck and run in the opposite direction.

Is there a soccer personality? Is it an inborn talent that is developed through hard work? Or can anyone play this game? That is the question I ask myself over and over as I try to turn myself into a soccer player. I don't know whether I've done it yet. Maybe I need to practice longer and harder. Or maybe I need more natural athletic ability. I wonder if I will succeed if I really start to love the game. Or will I love the game only if I succeed at it?

I have lots of questions and not many answers. But one thing I know: I'm going to be on the soccer field this week, doing my best.

Abby folded the newspaper and took another bite of waffle. Then she reached inside her backpack and pulled out her journal.

No one in Hayes family has said a word about disastrous soccer game. Are they being polite and tactful, or have they all suffered amnesia?

I guess my secret is out now. My SuperSisters know that I'm on the team. Isabel hasn't given me her speech about "barbaric sports," and Eva hasn't told me a thousand ways I need to improve myself. Has the article interrupted their usual train of thought? I hope so!

Jessica just called. Said that anyone can fall, but few people can make a goal. Especially someone who has been playing for a short time. She said she liked my article, too. Invited me to a sleepover on Saturday night with Natalie. Jessica's mother doesn't usually let her have sleepovers, but Jessica used great powers of persuasion. Told her mother that Natalie was new in town and hadn't been invited anywhere yet.

Natalie told her parents that Jessica and I are soccer players, so they are letting her sleep over.

Hooray! That's tomorrow night!

Am thinking about soccer goals.
1. Didn't give myself enough time.
2. Did pretty well for the time I had.
3. Have become much better player — if not great one or star yet.
4. Worked hard, did best. Should be proud of effort, not results.
5. Published article in newspaper.
6. Soccer season is not over yet!

Conclusion: Maybe there is a silver lining to every cloud! (Must apologize to whoever wrote that.) If I hadn't joined the team, I wouldn't have written the article or gotten published in the newspaper.

I wonder if Ms. Kantor will put it up on the bulletin board for everyone to see.

Father told me that I will receive fifteen dollars from *Journal* for my article. Will not spend money on soccer equipment. Will buy calculator to help with math problems instead.

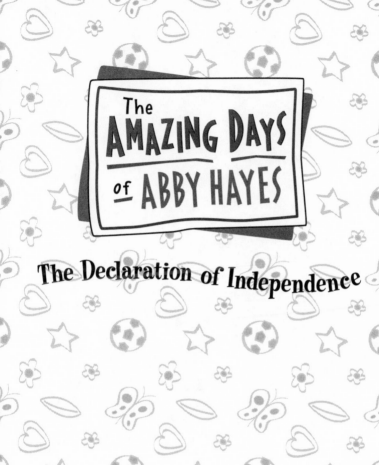

The AMAZING DAYS of ABBY HAYES

The Declaration of Independence

For Annika

Thanks to Jane for Web info,
to Max for tech support, and
to Mollie for enthusiasm and fifth-grade know-how.

Chapter 1

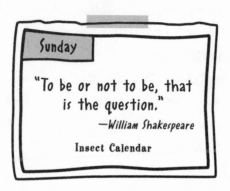

Sunday

"To be or not to be, that
is the question."
—William Shakespeare

Insect Calendar

To be <u>what</u> is the question. And <u>why</u> is another question. Why doesn't anyone ever ask that one?

Brianna is having a birthday party. She is inviting all the fifth-graders. It would be fun, except that we have to come in costume.

What shall I be? And why do I have to be anything but me?

When Abby Hayes joined her family in the living room, they were all in front of a blank television screen, while Alex, her seven-year-old brother, fiddled with the remote.

"Can you figure it out, Alex?" Eva demanded. Fresh from basketball practice, she paced up and down the living room, still in shorts and a jersey with number one emblazoned on the back.

Alex ignored her. Although he was only in second grade, he was a whiz in math and electronics; in his spare time, he put together computerized robots.

"Of course, he can figure it out!" Isabel, Eva's twin, exclaimed. She waved her fingernails, which she had just painted in five shades of violet, in the air. She was dressed in a long velvet skirt with matching Lycra top. There was a metal choker around her neck. "Alex knows what he's doing, don't you?"

"Mmmmph," Alex muttered. He pressed a button, and the screen turned blue, then went blank again.

"Abby, you got here just in time for the good part," her father joked, pointing to the empty screen. "I hope it's not too exciting for you."

Abby closed her eyes. "Tell me when the scary part is over!"

"Ha-ha, very funny," Eva said, doing jumping jacks in place.

Eva was the opposite of her twin in both style and personality. When she wasn't in sports clothes, she wore button-down shirts and neatly ironed jeans. And she never painted her nails.

On the couch, Abby's mother had spread out papers from her briefcase. Her reading glasses were perched on her nose. She had changed out of her tailored wool suit into sweatpants and a T-shirt.

"Mom, could you show up in court like that?" Abby asked. "In sweatpants and T-shirt?"

"Sure . . . of course." Her mother wasn't listening. She had to review a case before tomorrow morning. Sometimes Abby was tempted to write up her feelings in a legal brief and hand it to her mother just to get her undivided attention. But then she'd have to put a lot of "wherefores" and "thereuntos" and "hereunders" in her sentences, just like lawyers did.

Abby didn't want to write a lot of confusing words like that. Ms. Bunder, her favorite teacher, always said, "It's an art to write simple, clear sentences."

Maybe Ms. Bunder could do a creative writing class for lawyers, Abby thought. They needed one! She'd ask next time she saw her.

"Eva, will you stop that!" Isabel demanded as her sister jumped up and down, waving her arms and legs. "You look like a windmill."

"I'm increasing my respiration rate," Eva retorted. "The heart is a muscle. It needs to be exercised. You don't get exercise by painting your fingernails to match the wallpaper and sitting in the library all day."

"It's more important to exercise your mind!" Isabel shot back. "Mental concentration improves health and physical performance! You should know that, Eva. The best athletes work with the mind before the body."

"Oh, yeah?" Eva said.

Isabel was a champion debater, but that didn't stop Eva from arguing with her. She believed in the number one emblazoned on the back of her basketball jersey.

Abby sighed and sank down in her chair. She pulled out the purple journal that Ms. Bunder had given her the first day of creative writing class and opened it to a new page.

SuperSisters #1 and #2 are at it again. Mind versus matter. Or, as I read in my Genius Calendar, "What is matter? Never mind. What is mind? No matter." Ha-ha. That is a good quote. New friend Natalie bought me Genius Calendar last week. She moved here right before school started. She loves chemistry, mysteries, and Harry Potter books. (I wonder if there are other Potter heads in the fifth grade. I hope Natalie will not like them better than she likes me and Jessica.)

Decibel level of SuperSister argument has increased. Sonic boom about to happen. Father is ignoring screaming sisters. He is trying to help Alex get the VCR running again. Mother hears nothing. When roof 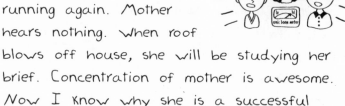 blows off house, she will be studying her brief. Concentration of mother is awesome. Now I know why she is a successful lawyer.

As for me, my journal is my best friend (aside from Jessica and maybe Natalie). Writing is a solace, as Ms. Bunder says.

 I looked up "solace" in Isabel's dictionary. It sounded slippery, like cod liver oil, which is a disgusting medicine that kids have to take in old-fashioned books. They all hate it! Thank goodness we don't have cod liver oil today. Solace means "alleviation of distress or discomfort." It is like medicine, but not nasty stuff like cod liver oil.

My journal is soothing and comforting like a cozy pillow or music at night. It's like my mother coming into my room when I'm sick and putting her hand on my forehead.

It's . . . uh-oh! Interruption! We interrupt this journal entry for an emergency announcement.

SuperSis Sonic Boom about to be heard. Isabel's face turning color of purple fingernails. Eva huffing and puffing, but not from exercise. Alex valiantly working to get VCR on track before house blows apart from force of sisters' galelike fury. Father smiling and pretending nothing is happening. Mother still reading brief. Is my journal sonic-boom proof????

Eva and Isabel faced off, screaming insults. Abby shut her journal and waited for the final explosion. It was impossible to write with all this noise, anyway.

"Come on, Alex, do your magic," Abby urged.

Her little brother bent over the controls. As usual, his hair was standing up on his head, and his shirt was buttoned wrong. He wore one green sock and one blue one.

Her father always said, "Let them work it out themselves," but even though Isabel and Eva had had fourteen years to work it out, they still hadn't.

If the television got fixed, the twins might be distracted from their fight. Nothing less would do it. If Abby tried to step in between her warring sisters, they'd squash her.

Only her seven-year-old brother could save the day.

Alex pointed the remote at the screen. Light appeared, and then music began to play. A picture of pumpkins flashed on the screen.

"Hooray, Alex!" Abby yelled.

Eva and Isabel paused in their fight. Their mother looked up from her brief.

"The switch at the back was set on channel four, not three," Alex explained.

"What are we watching, anyway?" Abby asked.

"Last year's Harvest Festival at the high school."

It was a Hayes family tradition to help out with

the festival. Last year Eva manned the prize booth and Isabel dressed up like a fortune-teller. Abby's mother raffled cakes, and her father let kids throw wet sponges at his face.

Abby took Alex around to all the games and activities he wanted.

"Look, look!" Alex pointed to the screen. In the midst of crowds of excited children bobbing for apples and getting their faces painted, a spaceship appeared. It flew crazily through the room, bounced off the gymnasium walls, and then abruptly disappeared.

"I don't remember any UFO's at the festival," their father said.

"I did it with the computer!" Alex cried. "It was easy!"

"Very cute, Alex," Abby said.

Their mother nodded. "I should get you to edit the videotapes of our annual board meetings. They could use a spaceship or two."

"When's the festival this year?" their father asked.

"In a month." Eva got up from the couch.

"Are we all going?" their mother asked.

"Yes!" the twins chimed.

Their father smiled. "It's nice to hear you two agree for a change."

"Abby, you'll take Alex again, right?" her mother said.

Abby took a deep breath. She loved her younger brother, and they did many things together. They played chess (not a lot, because she always lost), Rollerbladed, biked, and baked cookies together. When she was training hard for the soccer team, Alex had helped her out, even though he didn't know much about soccer.

It wasn't that she didn't want to be with Alex anymore, it was just that she wanted to be with her friends more. Next year she would be in middle school. She was old enough to go out more on her own, to have more independence.

Besides, the festival would be so much fun if she could wander around with her friends! There were games of skill, music, cotton candy, cakes, prizes, and crowds of people having a good time.

"I want to go with my friends," she announced. "I want to bike to the festival by myself with Natalie and Jessica."

Chapter 2

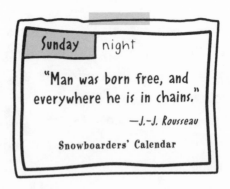

Sunday night

"Man was born free, and everywhere he is in chains."

—J.-J. Rousseau

Snowboarders' Calendar

Ha! That's for sure! I bet whoever wrote this knew my family.

And now your roving reporter, Abby Hayes, brings you the latest from the Hayes family.

News flash! A shocked silence greeted young Abby Hayes's Declaration of Independence in the Hayes living room. The bold fifth-grader announced to her family that she would no longer be the companion for Alex Hayes during this year's Harvest Festival at the high school.

"Ten-year-olds have the right to the pursuit of liberty, happiness, and pierced ears," she declared. "They do not have to take their little brothers everywhere."

"I'm not little!" Alex Hayes interrupted furiously.

Ignoring this interruption, Abby Hayes demanded the right to ride her bicycle to the festival with her fellow fifth-graders, Jessica and Natalie. She said that she wanted to have her face painted with butterflies without a second-grader waiting to be taken to the science booth. She announced that she no longer wanted to have her parents and older sisters accompany her everywhere.

The older Hayeses reacted with stunned disbelief. Paul Hayes, Abby's father, who often supports her when no one else does, expressed outrage and dismay.

"We were counting on you," he said. "We volunteered our time because we thought you would watch Alex. Now what are we going to do?"

Eva Hayes, star athlete and constant muscle flexer, said, "Why can't you take Alex with you? He has a bike! He can ride with you and your friends!"

Her fraternal twin, Isabel Hayes, pointed to Alex Hayes, who was frowning in the corner. "Look at the poor kid! He's so upset! How can you disappoint him like this?"

Only Olivia Hayes, who sometimes does not understand her ten-year-old daughter, spoke with the voice of reason. "Abby wants more freedom. That's only natural. However, she has to prove that she has the maturity to handle it. She has to take more responsibility. Can you do that, Abby?"

"Yes!" cried the young revolutionary.

After some discussion, her father agreed that this was fair. Isabel and Eva Hayes had to agree to change their schedules so they could take Alex Hayes to the festival. (They were not happy.)

Alex was not happy, either. "Isabel won't like it when I want to throw balls," he complained. "Eva will get bored at the science exhibits."

Paul Hayes tried to reassure his son. "Go to the science exhibit with Isabel and throw balls with Eva."

"Abby has always taken me. I want Abby and no one else!"

"We'll still do special things together,"

Abby Hayes promised him. "Maybe we can Rollerblade together this weekend."

Alex Hayes turned away and did not reply.

Olivia Hayes hugged him and told him that his sister was growing up.

"Does that mean I can get my ears pierced?" Abby Hayes asked quickly.

Olivia Hayes laughed and said no, but good try.

The family meeting broke up. Isabel Hayes returned to her studies. Eva Hayes resumed her calisthenics. Olivia Hayes put her glasses back on and returned to her brief. Paul Hayes went into the kitchen to clean up. Abby Hayes took her journal upstairs to write this news flash, while Alex Hayes repeated that he wasn't going to the festival without Abby.

Chapter 3

Tuesday | morning

"It takes one a long time
to become young."

—Picasso

Monuments of
Ancient Greece Calendar

I wish it took a short time to become old! If I were older, I wouldn't have to prove that I'm mature enough to go to the festival with my friends.

<u>Ways to Stun Family with Maturity</u>

Rescue Alex from burning building. (Must wait for burning building.)

Design Web page for Father's clients. (Must learn to use father's computer programs.)

Plead case for Mother in court. (Go to law school?)

Single-handedly save entire family from food poisoning. (Become doctor first. What if I have food poisoning, too? Forget about medical school. Call 911.)

These ideas too complicated and difficult. Must find something simpler but very impressive.

Think. Think. Think!

Make bed every morning.

Get own breakfast.

Put away clothes in-stead of leaving them on bed, chairs, desk, and floor.

(Aren't I supposed to do this stuff anyway?)

Don't whine when reminded to set table.

I'm happy to help.

Don't say "Do I have to?" or "Why me?" when asked to sweep kitchen floor.

BRAINSTORM!!! Parents are always complaining about all the work they do and how they never get enough help around the house from their children, who are too busy with sports and school and friends.

Do extra chores that no one wants to do!!!

My parents will be awed, impressed, and bowled over by my maturity and responsibility. They will let me go to the festival AND Paradise Pizza by myself with Natalie and Jessica. Maybe they will even let me get my ears pierced!

Alex banged on Abby's door. "Jessica's here to pick you up for school!" he called.

Abby's best friend entered the room. Jessica was tall, especially next to Abby. She had straight shiny brown hair and large brown eyes. She was wearing her favorite outfit of overalls decorated with peace signs and smile buttons and a striped sweater underneath. An asthma inhaler peeked out from one of her overall pockets. Even though she had asthma, Jessica didn't let it stop her from becoming a very good athlete. She had helped Abby improve her soccer game at the beginning of soccer season.

"Coming in, Alex?" Abby called. Her brother often joined the girls for a few minutes in the morning.

"No!" He stomped off.

"What's with him?" Jessica asked.

"Alex?" Abby shrugged. "He's mad that I'm not taking him to the festival."

"Friends are important, too," Jessica said.

"Yes," Abby said. Too bad Alex wasn't as understanding as Jessica.

"I'll make it up to him, though," she promised. "We'll do something special and unforgettable together."

"What?"

"I don't know, but it'll be good!" Abby opened her bureau drawer. She couldn't think too much about her little brother right now. She had other things on her mind.

"Look," she said to Jessica, holding her gold hoop earrings to her ears. "Don't these look good?"

"Yes," Jessica agreed.

"My ears just cry out for earrings!" Abby exclaimed. "They look so plain and boring without them!"

"I know," Jessica sighed. She, too, had been campaigning to get her ears pierced. "I saw silver spaceship earrings in the mall." Abby's best friend loved anything to do with outer space. She planned to be an astronaut when she grew up. "My mother wouldn't let me buy them."

"I bet she'll get them for you for your birthday," Abby said. "Remember? That happened last year with the globe you wanted."

Jessica smiled. "You're right! Maybe she's planning to let me get my ears pierced for my birthday. Every time I mention earrings, she mysteriously changes the subject."

"My mother does, too," Abby said. "Mostly because she's sick of me talking about earrings all the time."

Jessica glanced around the room. "Almost ready to go?"

"Almost." Abby returned the hoops to their box in her drawer. She smoothed her hand over her curly red hair one last time — not that it did any good — and picked up her backpack.

"Wait! I almost forgot!" She dashed over to the bed, smoothed down the blankets, fluffed up the pillow, and pulled the comforter neatly over everything.

Her friend stared at her. "Abby! You're making your bed?"

Jessica was a neat freak. Her desk was neat, her room was neat, her homework was neat, and her mind was neat, too.

Abby was the opposite. Normally her room, her thoughts, and her pages were as messy and wild as her hair.

"I'm proving to my family how mature I am," Abby said. "Otherwise they won't let me go to the festival with you. Lucky you that you have such an easy mother!"

"You know what she's like."

"And you don't have younger brothers or sisters, either," Abby said enviously.

"Alex is great," Jessica said. "I'd take him any day."

The two girls went downstairs.

In the kitchen, Abby's father was reading the paper. As usual, he was in his bathrobe and unshaved. He had been up since early in the morning, working in his home office, setting up Web pages for his clients and advising them on how to do business on the Web.

Alex was upstairs packing his backpack for school.

The twins had left half an hour ago, and her mother had gone to the office early.

"Hi, Dad," Abby said. She took a bagel from the counter, smeared some cream cheese on it, and headed toward the door. "Bye, Dad."

"Breakfast, Abby?" Her father pointed to a chair. "Ever considered sitting down for it? Jessica? Hungry for some of my special French toast?"

"I already ate," Jessica said. "Thanks anyway."

"This is my breakfast, Dad." Abby waved the bagel in the air, hoping that her father wouldn't (a) lecture her on the importance of a healthy, relaxed start to the day; or (b) insist that she eat his special French toast. "We're going early to school to put up fall decorations."

"Pumpkins? Corn? Squash?"

"Colored crepe paper," Jessica explained. "And block prints that we made last week in art class."

"Ah. Well, have a good day in school, girls."

"Bye, Dad!" Abby picked up her backpack and headed for the door. "I'll be home late! We have soccer practice after school!"

She snatched her blue bucket hat from the closet.

"Good-bye, Alex!" she called.

There was no answer.

"GOOD-BYE, ALEX!" she yelled again.

Still nothing.

Abby exchanged a worried glance with Jessica. Sometimes Alex got mad, but not usually this mad.

"He'll get over it," Jessica said.

She hoped Jessica was right. She didn't have any siblings. Sometimes Abby envied her. Not having younger brothers or older sisters might be the secret of Jessica's calm. Abby sometimes wondered if Jessica got lonely without anyone to tease, torment, or play with at home.

She would offer to play chess with Alex tonight. That would put him in a better mood.

He had to get over it. He didn't have a choice. Abby refused to go to the festival with her family this year. She was ten years old. She had to make her stand sometime.

Chapter 4

Wednesday

"Happiness is contagious."

Old Sneakers Calendar

Is this true? Then why isn't my family dancing with joy that I want to go to the festival with my friends?

Brianna is happy about her birthday party. She didn't stop talking about it at soccer practice yesterday. A lot of other kids are happy, too — but not me!

I don't know what kind of costume to wear. It's too much to think about when I have to concentrate every ounce of my energy on proving how mature I am.

<u>Abby's Grown-up (Groan-up!) List</u>

Made bed for fourth day in a row. Even Isabel does not make her bed every day! Wonder how many bed makings it will take to set world record. (Check <u>Guinness Book of World Records</u>.)

Picked up muddy soccer clothes from bedroom floor and put them in hamper.

Threw crumpled math homework in trash instead of stuffing it in my backpack.

Cleared dishes without being nagged. (Mother had to ask me ONLY twice.)

Played chess with Alex. Did not accuse younger brother of cheating even after he won seven games in a row. Did not sweep chess pieces off board in frustration. Did not stomp off in a fury.

Incredible restraint and self-control.

I am mature; I am very mature. Why hasn't anyone in my family noticed????? They act as if everything is normal!

At school, everyone was talking about Brianna's party. Especially Brianna.

"I'm going to have a live band at my party," Brianna announced at lunchtime. "We're going to have dancing and refreshments. It'll be *the* party of the fifth grade."

She tossed her long dark hair over her shoulder and put her hand on her hip. She was wearing a glitter slip dress with matching suede platform shoes. Her arms were bare, but she wasn't shivering.

Sitting a few feet away with Natalie and Jessica, Abby shivered at the sight of Brianna. Was Brianna cold? Or just cold-blooded? How could she wear a sleeveless dress at the end of October! Maybe she needed a calendar to remind her what month it was.

There was an idea for a birthday present! She could buy Brianna a calendar with lots of places to put her own picture. Or would she prefer a brag book?

Abby took a bite of the egg-salad sandwich she had made for her lunch. It was way too salty. She had gotten distracted by an argument between her sisters as she was making it.

"Her cousins are in the band," Brianna's best friend Bethany said. "They're in middle school!"

Like her best friend, Bethany was dressed in a short dress and platform shoes. Her long blond hair was tied in a ponytail.

At least she wore a cardigan over the dress, Abby thought. Bethany imitated almost everything Brianna did, but she drew the line at wearing summer clothes in autumn.

"My cousins are professionals," Brianna emphasized. "They play at birthday parties and get paid for it."

"Probably toddlers' parties," Abby whispered to Jessica and Natalie.

Brianna glanced at Zach. "We're also going to give out prizes for the best costumes. Like Most Beautiful."

"That's Brianna," Bethany interrupted.

Brianna smiled graciously. "Or Funniest Costume or Most Original. I think you should try for Most Original, Zach. Weren't you a computer keyboard last year for Halloween?"

Zach ignored her. He was bent over the electronic game he had snuck into school.

Abby slid her journal onto her lap and picked up her purple pen.

What does Brianna see in Zach, anyway?

Hair: blond. Eyes: blue. Lashes: long and dark. A nose. A mouth. A chin. The usual stuff.

His mind: obsessed by electronics. (When Zach was a baby, he was found on a doorstep and raised by loving computers. A hard drive saved his life in his early years.)

He also likes soccer, ice hockey, and basketball. His best friend is Tyler.

Conclusion: Zach looks and acts like every other fifth-grade boy.

Can't figure out why Brianna likes him. One of the great mysteries of the universe, like the pyramids or the Bermuda Triangle. Impossible to explain to a rational mind.

"What are you going to be for Brianna's party?" Jessica asked Natalie.

Abby took another bite of the salty egg-salad sandwich, then washed it down with fruit juice. "I bet you're going to be Harry Potter."

"My parents don't want me to go." Natalie was thin, with short black hair. She didn't seem to care what she wore; her clothes were dark and rumpled. Sometimes they had stains on them from the chemistry experiments she performed.

"Why not?" Abby and Jessica demanded at the same time.

"I can't figure out what they think. I'm either too young or too old!" Natalie twirled her spoon in her yogurt cup. "If I were in first grade, it would be okay. If I were in ninth grade, it would be okay. But I'm a fifth-grader, so it's not okay. I'm stuck in the middle!"

"That stinks!" Abby cried.

"Maybe they'll change their minds about Brianna's party," Jessica said.

"Maybe," Natalie echoed doubtfully.

Abby wondered if she should ask her parents to call Natalie's parents. Could they talk them into letting her go? Her mother might plead Natalie's case. It was handy to have a lawyer in the family. Abby would ask her later.

"What about the festival?" Abby said. "Jessica and I were hoping that you would bike over with us. Will your parents let you?"

"I'll meet you at the festival," Natalie said. "My mother is going to sell tickets. I'll have to go with her."

Jessica stood up. "I'm going to get some chocolate milk. Either of you want anything?"

"An ice-cream bar." Abby rummaged in her pocket for change. She ought to be saving her allowance for the festival, not spending it on extra desserts. She was still hungry, though. Her sandwich was too awful to eat. She pushed it away.

"Are you going to throw that out?" Zach asked. "If you are, I'll take it."

"It's nasty," Abby warned him.

Zach bit into the sandwich. "It's good," he said. "I love egg salad."

Zach actually likes it!!! Do boys have some kind of garbage disposal in their stomachs? They will eat anything.

That sandwich is so salty that Zach will float if he finishes it.

Must concentrate when making lunch tomorrow.

Do not get near salt shaker unless calm and focused.

Or else buy school lunch.

No, would rather bring my own. That way I can prove my maturity to parents AND pack two desserts.

Costume idea #1: Mixed-up Costume. A black cat's tail (first grade) with a witch's mask (second grade) and a ghost sheet (third grade) and long red fingernails from my vampire costume (fourth grade). Ha-ha! I will win award for Most Confusing Costume!

I hope Brianna does not expect us to dance with the boys. She keeps looking at Zach every time she mentions dancing.

The bell rang. Abby closed her notebook, threw out her juice carton, and returned to the classroom with her friends.

Chapter 5

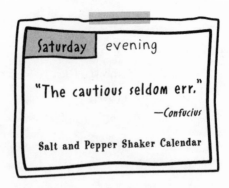

Saturday evening

"The cautious seldom err."
—Confucius

Salt and Pepper Shaker Calendar

The cautious seldom go to the Harvest Festival (or anywhere else) with their best friends.

Only the bold do what they want!

Asked Isabel the meaning of "err." (The word sounds like someone clearing their throat.) She said, "To make mistakes, like errors." I err all the time. But not about going to the festival with my friends!

<u>Abby's List of Bold Actions</u>
Continue to make bed, put dirty clothes in

hamper, throw out trash in wastebasket,
and clean up after myself.
 Clear table, even though it is Alex's week.
 Offer to make toast for father.
 Get mother's briefcase for work.
 Smile a lot. Even if my face hurts.

(Note: Checked <u>Guinness Book of World
Records</u>. There is no bed-making category.
Write letter to protest unfair policy. Or start
<u>Hayes Book of World Records</u> with cate-
gories for bed making, cheerful losing to
younger brothers, and longest unbroken record
for neat room kept by messy person.)

Family Reactions to Bold Actions
 What they're supposed to say:
 "Abby, we can't believe you're only ten
years old! You're acting like an adult!
You're so mature and
responsible that we've decided
to let you have everything you
want. Of course, you can bike
to the festival with your friends,
and don't forget to stop off at

Paradise Pizza on your way home. Here's a twenty-dollar bill. Have fun spending it. Be sure to get home by evening, because we're going to the mall to get your ears pierced."

What they could have said:
"Great effort, Abby! You're well on your way to getting permission to go to the festival with your friends."

What they did say:
"Thanks, Abby. Could you find my glasses? I put them down somewhere."

Was hoping that Plan A (for Action) would Amaze and Awe my parents. Since it hasn't, must move on to Plan B (for Bigger, Better, and Bolder).

Only the most heroic actions will impress Paul and Olivia Hayes. I must be fearless, brave, strong. Will take on nastiest of chores without flinching. Will clean bathroom sink. I might even tackle the tub.

Change of Subject (Thank Goodness)

In our creative writing class on Thursday morning, Ms. Bunder talked to us about haiku. They are Japanese poems with three lines and seventeen syllables. A lot of haiku poems are about nature. We don't have to write exactly seventeen syllables — just three lines. She said to try to write something surprising in the last line.

Zach raised his hand and asked if the surprise could be winning a million dollars.

Ms. Bunder smiled and said yes, if it fits into the poem.

"I wrote haiku poems in summer camp," Brianna said. "My mother had them framed and gave them to all our friends."

Bethany raised her hand. "I got one, Ms. Bunder! It's about Brianna dancing."

Brianna said it would be hard to decide what to write about: her birthday party, dancing, or being soccer captain.

Jessica said she is going to write about looking at the planets.

Natalie is still deciding whether to write about Harry Potter again. She has already used him for the subject of six creative writing assignments. "Time to switch to chemistry poems," she said.

I wonder what I will write about.

Before Abby had a chance to write anything else, there was a knock at the door.

Eva entered Abby's bedroom. She sat down on the neatly made bed and gazed at the clean, vacuumed rug. Then she stared at the many calendars lining the walls, particularly Abby's favorite, the Spuds Calendar. She shook her head, sighed, then turned to her younger sister.

"Abby, will you do me a favor?"

Abby folded her arms. A tough, no-nonsense expression settled on her face. "What?" she demanded.

"I want to go to a hockey game tonight, but I have to clean the bathroom first."

"So?"

"I thought you could do it."

"Me? I don't clean bathrooms."

Abby wasn't going to let on that she had been planning to clean the bathroom that very night. She certainly wasn't going to reveal to her older sister that she had already taken a pair of rubber gloves and a sponge from the kitchen.

"Can't you do something for me?" Eva cried. "I'm bringing Alex to the festival while you run around with your friends!"

"Oh, right. Okay, I'll do it."

"Thanks, little sis. You're the best." Eva stood up to leave. "The cleaning stuff is under the sink," she reminded her. "Don't forget to polish the faucets!"

Note to self: A lucky break! Might have done Eva's work without knowing it. In future, make sure am not doing SuperSibs' chores when trying to prove maturity to parents!

Haiku Poems

1.

Wiping the bathroom sink
My hands wet with foaming cleanser.
Did someone coat the basin with
  dirt and mud?

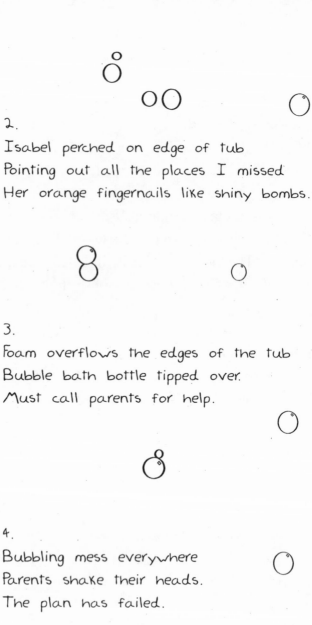

2.

Isabel perched on edge of tub
Pointing out all the places I missed
Her orange fingernails like shiny bombs.

3.

Foam overflows the edges of the tub
Bubble bath bottle tipped over.
Must call parents for help.

4.

Bubbling mess everywhere
Parents shake their heads.
The plan has failed.

Chapter 6

Why???

The world has too many questions and not enough answers!

My Parents' Questions

Why was the tub full of bubbles?

Why didn't I turn off the water before the bubbles started to go over the edge of the tub?

How come I used good towels to clean the mess up?

What was I doing in the bathroom, anyway? Wasn't it Eva's week to clean?

My Questions

Who forgot to tighten the cap on the bottle of bubbles?

. How was I supposed to know that it wasn't a good idea to turn on the faucets full force to wash the bubble stuff down the drain?

So what if they were "good" towels? Was I supposed to let bubbles keep pouring onto the floor while I searched for "bad" ones?

If those towels are so special, how come Eva and Isabel use them?

Why do these things always happen to me? (Is it the red hair? Or the weird gene that skipped the rest of my family and picked me?)

Scratch out Plans A and B. On to Plan C: for Creative? or for Convincing? Hope I do not have to go through the entire alphabet before my parents let me bike to the festival. I will be eighty by the time I get to Z.

Plan C will not involve water or soap.

Abby tiptoed downstairs. Her family was still sleeping. For once, she was the first one up. Her bed was made, her room was neat, and she was now about to make breakfast for the entire family.

This was one for the *Hayes Book of World Records*, she thought. "Earliest Rising on a Sunday Morning by Fifth-Grader."

The phone rang. Abby grabbed it.

"Hi, Jessica," she whispered.

"Are you up?" her friend asked.

"Sure. I've been up for an hour." Abby sniffed the air. It still smelled like bubble bath. Soon the smell of delicious pancakes would make her family forget all about last night's disaster. This time, her plan wasn't going to fail. Jessica, who was a good cook, was going to help her.

"Shall I come over?" Jessica asked.

"Sure," Abby whispered. "Remember: Plan C for Cooking."

"I'll be there in five minutes."

Abby went to the kitchen. She got out the pancake mix and the eggs. She found the measuring cup and measuring spoons. She took out the butter and maple syrup.

The back door opened. Jessica came in. She was bundled up in a coat and scarf. Her cheeks were red. "It's really cold outside." She wheezed as she spoke. "I wonder if it's going to snow. I bet they won't cancel the soccer game this afternoon."

She pulled out her asthma inhaler, aimed it at her mouth, and breathed in deeply. Then she glanced around the room. "Pancake mix? No way!"

"It's fast," Abby said. "It's good, too. Isabel makes pancakes from it all the time."

"I hate that stuff." Jessica cooked a meal for her mother and herself once a week. "I make pancakes from scratch."

Scratch? It sounded like chickens rooting around in the dirt. It sounded like one of Abby's messy math papers, where she had to cross everything out. It sounded like an itch or a bug bite.

It didn't sound like golden brown pancakes with butter and maple syrup.

"Are you sure?" Abby spoke carefully. She didn't

want to hurt Jessica's feelings. After all, she had come over at 7:30 A.M. on a Sunday morning to help Abby out. How many friends would do that? "I really need to impress my family. Especially after last night."

"This will do it," Jessica assured her. "Believe me, if they're used to pancakes from a mix, they'll go crazy over these."

"Crazy," Abby repeated doubtfully. "They already think I'm crazy."

"Don't worry. This will do the trick," Jessica promised. "Get out the baking powder, milk, flour, and sugar. If you have any fruit, we can throw that in, too."

Abby rummaged through the cupboards, pulling out boxes and cans and jars. Jessica found some mixing bowls and began to measure out flour and sugar.

Half an hour later, as the first pancakes were beginning to cook, Alex wandered into the kitchen. As usual in the morning, his hair stood straight up on his head. His pajama tops and bottoms did not match. He wore an old pair of slippers and carried a battered computer keyboard under his arm.

"What are you doing with that keyboard, Alex?"

Jessica asked. She was sitting at the table, leafing through a cookbook, while Abby flipped pancakes.

"Taking it apart," he said. "I want to see what's inside."

"Do you want pancakes?" Abby asked. "They're Jessica's special recipe."

"Okay." He yawned and shuffled over to the table.

"Are you still mad at Abby?" Jessica asked.

Alex made a face. "Naw."

Every day Alex seemed a little more friendly and a little less hurt. The thaw was slow but sure.

"Do you want blueberries in your pancakes?" Abby asked.

"Okay." He yawned again.

Abby sprinkled frozen berries into the batter, then spooned it onto the hot pan. She watched as the batter began to bubble, then flipped the pancakes to the other side the way Jessica had instructed her.

"Here, Alex," she said, handing him a plate. "Don't pour out half the bottle of maple syrup."

Alex grunted and reached for the comics.

The Hayes family members began to drift into the kitchen.

"What smells so good?" Abby's mother asked sleepily.

Sunday was the only day of the week on which Olivia Hayes slept past 6:30 A.M. In honor of the occasion, she wore her old blue terry bathrobe and a pair of fuzzy slippers that Abby had made her in fourth grade. "Do I smell coffee, too?"

"Yes!" Abby said. "Welcome to the Hayes-y Days Café!"

Eva came in, pulling a sweatshirt over her swimsuit. "Pancakes!" she exclaimed. "That's great. I have a meet in an hour and a half. This is just what I need."

Abby beamed. Her plan was working. Everyone in her family was thrilled. The pancakes were turning out perfectly. She hoped she and Jessica had made enough for everyone — including themselves. She couldn't wait to try a few!

"By the way, Abby," Eva continued, "that tub was sparkling. How did you do it? You really amaze me. She cleaned the bathroom last night, Mom."

"Yes, I know." Abby's mother looked up from the newspaper.

"I think she should do it more often." Eva smiled at Abby. "It smells really good in there, too."

Abby flushed. This was the last thing she needed — Eva reminding everyone of last night's disaster.

Jessica came to the rescue. "Does anyone want hot chocolate?" she said loudly. "I'll heat up some milk!"

"Me!" Alex yelled.

"Me, too," said her father, coming into the kitchen. He had on sweatpants and a sweatshirt. While Abby's mother said that Sunday was her lazy day to sleep late and read the paper, her father liked to jog first thing in the morning. "I'll take some with my coffee. Who made this wonderful breakfast?"

"We're eating at the Hayes-y Days Café," Abby's mother said with a smile. "Jessica and Abby are the chefs."

"It was Abby's idea," Jessica said.

"I couldn't have done it without Jessica," Abby said.

"Done what?" Isabel made a grand entrance, as she often did. She wore a long yellow skirt and a V-neck T-shirt. A silver necklace with blue glass flowers was around her neck. She had painted her fingernails yellow to match her skirt.

All Isabel needed, Abby thought, was a crown on her head and a scepter in her hand.

"They got up early and made breakfast," Abby's father said. "That's impressive, isn't it?"

Impressive. That was the word Abby had been

waiting to hear. "It's mature, too, Dad," she reminded him. "And responsible."

"What happened to the bubble bath?" Isabel interrupted, spearing a pancake with her fork. "I wanted to take a long, hot bath this morning but had to take a shower instead."

"Bubble bath?" Abby repeated.

She should have known that just when everything was going well, one of her SuperSibs would spoil it.

Last night, Isabel made a pain of herself by hovering over Abby and pointing out all the places she had forgotten to clean. Then she left for a play with her friends, missing the Great Bathtub Disaster.

Yet Isabel still brought it up! Did she have some kind of sisterly radar that allowed her to home in on the most painful subjects?

"Um, the bottle tipped over when I was cleaning the bathroom," Abby mumbled.

Jessica shot her a sympathetic look.

"The whole thing?" Isabel demanded.

Abby nodded. She wished she had been able to save just a capful of the horrid stuff. Then Isabel would have been soaking in the tub at this very minute, instead of embarrassing her in front of the entire Hayes family.

"Why were you cleaning the bathroom, anyway, Abby? I meant to ask you last night. It's Eva's turn, isn't it?"

"She was doing it as a favor to me," Eva said. "I'm watching Alex during the festival, you know."

"You made her clean the bathroom for you because of that?" Isabel demanded.

Eva's eyes narrowed, and her chin thrust forward stubbornly. "Yeah, I did. So what?"

"Don't take advantage," Isabel pronounced. "You should be ashamed of yourself. What's the big deal about taking Alex to the festival, anyway? I'm doing it."

Alex, who had been immersed in the comics, suddenly let out a piercing wail. "I don't want Eva and Isabel to take me to the festival! I want Abby!"

Eva and Isabel ignored him.

"Ashamed of myself? For what?" Eva spat. "She practically begged me to clean the bathroom! Right, Abby?"

"Wrong," Abby answered, but fortunately no one was listening. When the two SuperPowers of the Hayes family engaged in battle, the best tactic was to remain silent and invisible.

"Abby! Abby! I want Abby!"

The twin SuperSibs faced off, screaming insults to the background music of Alex's wail.

Their father shook his head and disappeared out the door. Their mother picked up her newspaper and coffee and went to sit in the living room, muttering about her one day of peace.

Abby turned off the stove and slowly backed out of the kitchen. Jessica followed her.

"I wish I was an only child!" Abby said.

Jessica nodded her head in sympathy.

The breakfast had been perfectly made. The pancakes were heavenly. The coffee and hot chocolate were excellent. But the fighting twins had spoiled it all. Now Alex was upset again, and her parents had been reminded several times of last night's disaster. All of Abby's hard work had been undone.

Chapter 7

Tuesday

"Anger is a short madness."
—Horace

Hat Calendar

Sometimes it's a long one. Alex wouldn't speak to me until breakfast on Monday. The twins were fighting when I left and fighting when I came home. Did they fight all day? Eva had a swimming match, so they had to stop for a few hours.

After cleaning up the kitchen, Jessica and I went over to her house (certified sibling free). We played soccer in the afternoon, and our team won. I almost made a

Certified Sibling Free

point! It was freezing on the field! But better than being at my house.

I wanted to stay at Jessica's for a week, but I had to go home and think up Plan D.

Plan C was Catastrophic, Cataclysmic, and Calamitous. All these words point to Disaster. That is <u>not</u> what I want for Plan D.

Plan D must be Daring, Decisive, and Dynamic.

Hayes Book of World Records

A. Hayes has continued her quest for the world record in Uninterrupted Bed Making (sixteen days), as well as Neat Room Kept by a Messy Person (more than two weeks), and the special Good Loser Award When Playing Chess with Boy Genius (twenty-five games). In addition, she is trying for the record for Most Promising Plan That Completely Flopped (Sunday's breakfast).

(Shall I add a category for Longest Time to Decide on a Costume for Fifth-Grade Birthday Party? I might win that one, too!)

Costume idea #2: Be invisible.

This is what Natalie should be. Then she could go to Brianna's birthday party with Jessica and me. I asked my mother to talk to her mother, but she said that every family had its own rules, and we couldn't tell other families what to do.

Natalie's family's rules are unfair! I told Natalie about my Declaration of Independence, but she shook her head and said it wouldn't work in her family. It would just make things worse.

She is embarrassed because she is the only person in the fifth grade who can't go — just because it's a boy-girl party. She asked Jessica and me not to tell ANY-ONE!

We told her we would guard her secret with our lives. (Question: How do lives guard a secret? I don't understand.)

At least Natalie can meet us at the festival.

Speaking of the festival, my father said

this morning, "You're trying hard, Abby, and your mother and I appreciate it."

"Does that mean I have permission to bike to the festival?"

"Not yet," he said, "but keep up the good work."

First sign that Plans A, B, and C have not been complete failures. Must put renewed effort into Plan D.

I said to my father, "Everyone in my class is going on their own. Jessica, Brianna, Bethany, Zach, Tyler, Rachel, Meghan, and Jon are all going to the festival by themselves and with their friends. They don't have to prove how mature they are, either. Their parents just know!"

(I didn't mention Natalie.)

My father answered, "You still have to show us that you're responsible enough to be trusted on your own."

Natalie, Jessica, and I took a vote and decided that Jessica has the best family situation. She has no siblings and only one parent, who is not too strict.

Natalie told us that she has an older brother. We were surprised because she has never mentioned him before. He doesn't live with her family except on vacations and in the summer. He goes to boarding school. His name is Nicholas. She said he is even more annoying than the twin SuperSibs. That is hard to imagine.

"Everybody get out paper and pencil for the math quiz," Ms. Kantor announced.

Abby groaned. She hated math, and especially math quizzes. They were just too hard! Alex, on the other hand, could do math problems in his sleep, and probably did. Isabel got great marks in everything. When the fairy godmother handed out math genes in the Hayes family, she had skipped Abby's cradle. Abby couldn't figure out how she had missed her! Her red hair was like a flashing light.

She raised her hand. "Ms. Kantor? How come we have so many math quizzes?"

Ms. Kantor cleared her throat. "To prepare you for the statewide math tests at the end of the year."

"In third grade, I placed in the ninety-eighth percentile," Brianna said. She glanced at Zach. "That's nationwide."

"Yay, Brianna," Bethany said.

If there was a national bragging standard, Brianna would be in the one-hundredth percentile.

"I hate those state tests," Abby muttered.

"All right, no more discussion," Ms. Kantor said. "I want all of you to score in the ninety-ninth percentile by the end of the year. That includes you, Abby. I know you can do it." She passed out the quizzes.

Abby stared at the sheet full of fractions and ratios.

Fortunately, she had studied the night before.

Unfortunately, she had already forgotten everything she studied.

When it came to math, her brain was like a colander. Math facts ran through it like water.

Natalie and Jessica were bent over their work. So were Brianna and Bethany, Zach and Tyler, and most of the rest of the class.

"Concentrate! Concentrate!" Abby told herself sternly. She couldn't bring home a failing mark in math. Her parents wouldn't consider it a sign of maturity and responsibility.

She began to multiply and divide. When Ms. Kantor collected the tests, she had finished all the problems but one.

"That's the way, Abby!" Ms. Kantor said. "Good work!"

Abby tried to smile. Just because she had finished the quiz didn't mean she had gotten the right answers.

Ms. Kantor walked to the blackboard. Her long skirt swished around her ankles. She was wearing sneakers and ankle socks. They weren't fashionable like Ms. Bunder's combat boots, but Ms. Kantor said they were comfortable. "Okay, let's go over our spelling words now," she announced. "Any volunteers to give me a sentence with 'fragile'? Jessica?"

Jessica stood up. "The environment is very fragile."

"Good," Ms. Kantor said. "The next word is 'absolutely.' Bethany?"

"Brianna's birthday party will be absolutely the best," Bethany said.

Bethany's answer was absolutely obvious, Abby thought. She glanced over at Natalie who was scribbling on her social studies notebook. She wished that the B/Bs would stop talking about the party. Every time they did, Natalie looked upset.

"Abby?" Ms. Kantor said. "Can you give me a sentence with the word 'resistance'?"

"Um, yes." Abby stared at the blackboard. This is what happened when she didn't pay attention in class. She hoped that Ms. Kantor wouldn't send a note home about it.

"Resistance," she said slowly. "Parents have too much resistance to giving their kids freedom."

"Very good!" Ms. Kantor beamed at her.

Abby breathed a sigh of relief. Sometimes things worked out even when she wasn't trying hard.

If only it would happen that way with her family! One morning she would come down to breakfast, and her parents would announce that they were giving her permission to go to the festival with her friends. No more beds to make or tubs to scrub or chess games to be suffered with Alex. Nothing further to prove.

Why couldn't everything be as easy as making up sentences?

Chapter 8

Thursday

"What you can do, or think
you can do, begin it."

—*Goethe*

Egret Calendar

Do I have to finish it, too?

   Things I have begun in the last few days:

taking out garbage,
sorting bottles,
cans, and
cardboard
for recycling,
organizing summer clothes to
put upstairs in attic,
vacuuming living room floor

Things I have finished:
my homework

Costume idea #3: The "I Forgot to Get a Costume" Costume. Go as yourself. Act like this is an original idea.

<u>The Roving Reporter in the Schoolyard</u>
News flash! Today at recess, Abby Hayes did a survey of her classmates on the back playground.

"What are your favorite techniques to get what you want from your parents?" our investigating journalist asked. "Please share them with your fellow fifth-graders for the good of humankind."

The following are the results of her survey.

Begging, whining, and pouting: 3 (extremely annoying to parents)

Yelling and throwing fits: 1 (This can backfire.)

Arguing: 12 (a clear majority)

Sulking in room: 3 (not always fun)

"Everyone else does/has it": 7 (Parents are on to this argument, but we all use it anyway.)

Nagging: 2 (Doing this until parents give in requires great strength of character.)

Did you know that Ms. Kantor's fifth-graders had such a range of talents? Every single fifth-grader has mastered all of these difficult methods. These so-called "kids" are able to switch techniques with lightning swiftness. They often work best in combination.

Brianna revealed her version of the one, two, three knockout. "First I ask. If that doesn't work, I pout. Then I throw a screaming fit. That always does it."

Brianna (B for Best) then demonstrated her pout. It was indeed world-class. If there was a Pouting Olympics, Brianna would take the gold medal.

When arguing with her mother, Jessica has taken the words "why?" and "because" to new heights.

When Zach wants something, he doesn't stop talking about it until he gets it.

Bethany demonstrated her tearful, wide-eyed look, which changes to sullen fury in an instant.

Only Natalie admitted that none of these methods work for her.

The investigative reporter is now investigating whether she can apply these methods to her own situation. Should she try to wear her parents down, throw a screaming fit, or sulk for hours to get permission to go to the festival on her own? No, perhaps not. Paul and Olivia Hayes would not consider this mature behavior.

Thursday was always Abby's favorite day of the week. If she had her way, she would color it purple. That was the day that Ms. Bunder came to teach creative writing to Ms. Kantor's fifth-graders.

Nothing could ever make Thursday into a bad day!

"Did everyone write haiku poems?" Ms. Bunder asked soon after she arrived in the classroom.

"Yes!" the class responded.

"Let's put them on the board," Ms. Bunder suggested. She was wearing wide-legged pants of a shiny gray material and a beaded shirt. Thin silver wires with blue-and-green glass beads hung around her neck. Sometimes Abby couldn't believe that she was a teacher and not a classmate of Isabel or Eva's.

"Did anyone write about nature?" Ms. Bunder asked.

Abby raised her hand. "I wrote about the Great Bathtub Disaster," she said. "A disaster is natural, isn't it? It involved lots of water."

"Okay, Abby, you may put your poems on the board."

When she was done, Brianna raised her hand. "Ms. Bunder! I wrote about playing soccer."

"I wrote a poem about Brianna," said Bethany. "Also about my hamster."

Ms. Bunder motioned them up to the board.

Rain and mud do not stop me
I am the captain
I am the best.

by Brianna

Next to her, Bethany wrote:

Squeak, squeak
Hamster runs around on his wheel
He keeps me up at night.

I am Brianna's best friend.
She is the coolest.
Yay, Brianna.

Jessica leaned toward Abby. "I like Bethany's poem about the hamster but not the one about Brianna," she whispered.

"Maybe she should switch the words 'hamster' and 'Brianna,'" Abby whispered back.

One by one, the other students went up and copied their poems on the board. Then they returned to their seats.

Ms. Bunder nodded as she read them. "This is a very creative class," she said. "Does anyone have any comments?"

Brianna raised her hand.

"Yes, Brianna?"

"I like Zach's poem." She giggled. "It's so . . . poetic!" In a dramatic voice, Brianna recited:

"The screen flickers.
Lights flash.
I am happy."

"Do you want to talk about your poem, Zach?"
Ms. Bunder asked.

Zach stood up. "It's about turning on the computer." He sat down again.

"I'd like to print that in my family newsletter," Brianna said.

Zach shook his head.

"Why not?" Brianna demanded.

"You can print mine, Brianna," Bethany said.

Brianna ignored her best friend. "I want Zach's!"

"No," Zach said. "Sorry."

Abby opened her journal.

If Brianna put Zach's poem in her family newsletter, would she say that he's her boyfriend? Probably. I don't think Zach would like that. No wonder he said no.

Is Brianna going to pout to make him give her his poem? No. Pouting is for parents, not for friends. She looks mad, though.

Doesn't Zach get bored thinking and talking and writing about computers all the time? And why does Brianna think he's so cute?

Natalie says it's Zach's blue eyes and blond hair. Jessica says it's because he's the only boy in the class who ignores Brianna. Now Bethany is starting to like Tyler. Is it because he is the best friend of her best friend's crush?

When Ms. Bunder said what a creative class we were, she looked right at me! She must have liked my poems about the Great Bathtub Disaster!

Abby's Wish List

I wish Ms. Bunder were my teacher for EVERY subject. (Even though I like Ms. Kantor, too.)

I wish I could write about making my bed or putting away my clothes instead of doing it.

I wish I could write to prove to my parents how mature I am!

I wish I could write a costume for Brianna's party.

Maybe I should go to Brianna's birthday
party as a poem! Ha-ha (costume idea #4).

After everyone had finished reading the poems,
Ms. Bunder collected them. "We'll write more," she
promised. "At the end of the year we'll choose our
best work and put it into a book. Maybe we can
have a poetry reading for your families."

"Yes!" Abby said, pumping her fist.

It would be a chance for her family to see her
shine. After all, this was her best subject, her favorite
class, and her most-loved teacher. Too bad she had to
wait until spring for it to happen!

Chapter 9

Thursday evening

"Do the work you love and love the work you do."

This isn't from a calendar. It's one of my mom's favorite sayings. I hear it all the time!

My mom loves her work. She has wanted to be a lawyer since she was nine. Dad loves his work, too, even though he was more than thirty when he started it.

(Were there personal computers around when Dad was a kid? He says no. I wonder if Zach and Tyler know how lucky they are? If they had been born a few years earlier, they would have missed computers. Then what would they have done?)

* * *

If adults love their work, why can't kid work be fun, too?

List of household chores I enjoy:

Okay. Never mind.

Hayes Household Update

At dinner tonight, Isabel Hayes lectured about checks and balances. (Note: Certain members of the Hayes family thought she was discussing a bank account. She was  actually talking about the federal government.)

Eva Hayes, captain of swim team, basketball team, and lacrosse team, said her teams will sponsor an auction at the festival. Prizes will be donated by families and businesses. Olivia Hayes will donate an hour of free legal advice.

Abby Hayes would like to win it. She would like to sue her family for the right to go to the festival.

Paul and Olivia Hayes have not yet made up their minds. The festival is only two weeks away!!!

The Hayes family will be very busy this weekend. On Saturday, Olivia Hayes will run a marathon race to raise money for sick children.

Paul Hayes will be out of town all weekend on important business.

Isabel Hayes has a debate, and Eva Hayes has a swim meet.

That leaves Abby and Alex Hayes. They have no particular activities.

Olivia Hayes must find someone to watch them.

After dinner, Abby helped her mother stack the dishes in the dishwasher.

"Wow!" she said, almost dropping a plate as the idea roared through her.

As brainstorms went, it was not a one or two. It

wasn't a skimpy, puny, thunder-and-lightning brain-storm. It was a full-fledged, gale-force, number-ten hurricane that blew everything away. "Mom, I have a solution to all your problems!"

"What?" her mother said.

"Since I don't have a soccer game this weekend, I can baby-sit for Alex on Saturday."

"You, Abby?"

"Yes, me. I'm ten years old and in fifth grade," Abby announced, as if her mother didn't know. She did, but sometimes it was good to remind her. "If I take care of Alex, you won't have to find a baby-sitter."

Abby's mother gave her a searching look. "Do you think you can do it? You'll have to watch him, enter-tain him, and feed him for an entire afternoon. You can't quit if you get tired or bored or annoyed."

"I won't," Abby promised. "Aren't I used to play-ing with Alex? I can fix peanut butter and jelly sand-wiches and take him to the park if the weather is good. If it isn't, we'll do projects at home."

"Will you watch him carefully?"

"Mom! I know the rules of safety. I won't answer the door or tell strangers that we're home alone. I'll make sure that Alex doesn't play with matches, or use the stove, or cross the street by himself."

Her father came into the kitchen with a cup of coffee.

"What do you think, Paul?" her mother asked. "Should we allow Abby to watch Alex this Saturday?"

Abby held her breath.

He took a sip of coffee. "All by herself?"

"I'll check in with the neighbors," Abby said. "And I can call Jessica's mom if I need help."

"It's not a bad idea," her father said. "How much do you charge?"

She thought for a moment. "A dollar fifty an hour. That's what Jessica gets when she baby-sits for the kids next door."

"What a bargain," her father said, winking at her.

Her mother nodded her head.

"And if I'm mature enough to watch Alex, you have to let me go to the festival with my friends," she added quickly.

Her parents exchanged glances.

"Sounds fair to me," her father said.

"Agreed," her mother said. "You have a deal."

HOORAY!! HOORAY!! No more horrible household chores! No more Great Bathtub Disasters or Battling Breakfasts! No more worrying about how to prove I'm trustworthy and mature! I can baby-sit, and get permission to go to the festival, AND get paid, too!

Plan E stands for Excellent, Exceptional, and Exactly What Is Needed.

Things I Promised to Do with Alex When Baby-Sitting

Rollerblading, biking, picnicking in the park (if it's not too cold), computer games, chess, reading his favorite books out loud for as long as he likes, and letting him take down all my calendars to play with.

"So?" he said.

Alex Hayes is not cooperating.
It is not fair.

* * *

"We can make brownies together," I finally promised, "and we'll put ice cream sundaes on top of them. With cherries, nuts, and chocolate candies."

"Okay," Alex said. "You win."

"I just want us to have fun together," I said.

Is this what it's like to be a parent? Arguing is exhausting. No wonder mothers and fathers are so tired all the time!

Alex and I will have fun together. My parents will be grateful. I will earn money and go to the festival with my friends.

(Repeat one hundred times at dawn, dusk, and midnight.)

Chapter 10

Friday

"To thine own self be true."
—*William Shakespeare*

Cornflake Calendar

Oh, yeah? You can't be true to yourself if you're a ten-year-old. You have to do what everyone tells you to do! Or else you're in big trouble.

Costume ideas #5, #6, #7, #8: Go as a zero. Go as a world record. Go as a gold record. Or a record company. Go as a lightbulb (for ideas). Go as. . . . Oh, go get a snack!

New Category for the <u>Hayes Book of</u> <u>World Records</u>: Most Costume Ideas for Brianna's Birthday Party.

Also, Most Throwaway Costume Ideas for Brianna's Birthday Party.

<u>What I Am Doing to Get Ready for</u>
<u>Baby-sitting Alex This Weekend</u>

Hid brownie mix so no one will use it before tomorrow.

Pushed ice cream to back of freezer so Isabel won't eat it tonight.

Found cherries, whipped cream, and nuts. Hid them.

Gathered Rollerblades, knee and wrist pads, and helmets into one pile.

Unlocked bikes.

Started using throat lozenges. Vocal cords must be in fine shape for nonstop reading.

Deep knee bends and push-ups.

Say "Alex, honey" every chance I get. Ruffle his hair. Smile at him a lot.

195

It was the end of the school day. Ms. Kantor's fifth-grade class put on their jackets, shouldered their backpacks, and got in line at the door.

"Hey, quit pushing me," Tyler said to Zach.

"I didn't do it," Zach protested.

Bethany giggled. She was wearing a white fleece pullover and a short embroidered skirt. "It was me. I bumped into you by accident. Sorry."

"Oh," Tyler said. He fiddled with a strap on his backpack. "Hey. I've been meaning to ask you. What's your hamster's name?"

"Blondie," Bethany said. "Do you like hamsters?"

"Sure," Tyler replied. "They're furry."

Bethany giggled again. "What are you doing after school?"

"You promised to come over to my house, Bethany," Brianna interrupted. She had on a pale blue peacoat over a dark red skirt. "We have to go over the party plans. The entire fifth grade is coming."

At the back of the line, Abby nudged Natalie. "Does Brianna know yet?" she whispered.

"No," Natalie whispered back. "I keep hoping my parents will change their minds."

"What if they don't?" Jessica asked.

"I'll pretend I'm sick," Natalie said.

Abby zipped up her jacket. She wished Natalie could go to the party. It just wasn't fair!

"Make up a good disease," she advised Natalie. "Maybe you can come down with Purple Lightning Madness that causes you to read Harry Potter books over and over again."

Natalie ran her hands through her short black hair and smiled. "That's what I'll be doing on the day of the party, reading Harry Potter books."

"Did someone say Harry Potter?" Zach asked. "I just started the first book. It's great!"

"It was me," Natalie said.

"Have you read them all?" he asked her.

"Fourteen times each," she replied.

"That's awesome," he said.

The bell rang. School was over for the week. The fifth-graders began to rush into the hallway.

"One at a time! Quietly!" Ms. Kantor called. She stood at the door and said good-bye to each student as they left.

"Have a great weekend," she said to Abby.

"I'm baby-sitting my little brother all Saturday afternoon."

"That's a lot of responsibility," Ms. Kantor said.

"I can handle it," Abby said.

As the fifth-graders spilled out onto the play-ground, Brianna gathered a circle of her classmates around her.

"Has everyone figured out their costumes?" she demanded. "The party's only nine days away."

"Nope," Abby said, yanking her bucket hat over her ears. It had gotten colder while they were in school. She hated when the days got colder instead of warmer.

Brianna turned to Zach and Tyler. "What about you two?"

"I'm not telling," Zach said.

"Me, neither," Tyler echoed.

"Natalie?" Brianna asked. "I hope you're planning something good. You've never been to one of my parties before. It'll be a real treat for you."

Natalie shuffled her feet. "I'm planning something very special," she mumbled.

"Like what?" Bethany said. "Tell us."

"It's a . . . it's a . . ." Natalie glanced desperately around the playground. "It . . . it . . ."

"It's a three-part costume," Jessica jumped in. "She's going with me and Abby. We're going to be . . ."

"Three links of a chain," Abby finished.

Brianna looked confused. "Three links of a chain? What kind of a costume is that?"

"Just a joke," Abby said. "We're really going to be a fork, knife, and spoon." It was the first thing out of her mouth. She hadn't thought about it at all.

"That's funny," Bethany said.

"It's easy to make, too," Abby said. Come to think of it, it was a pretty good idea. "You just need lots of aluminum foil and duct tape. And some cardboard."

"I'm going to spend all weekend working on my costume," Brianna said. "I bet everyone else will, too."

Natalie tried to smile.

"Me, too!" Bethany chirped. "Yay for Brianna's party!"

On the way home, Natalie thanked Abby and Jessica for keeping her secret. "But what will Brianna say when I don't show up?" she worried. "She expects a knife, fork, and spoon. What if only a knife and a spoon arrive at the party?"

"I'll tell her we forgot to wash you," Abby said. "You got left in the sink."

Natalie laughed.

"Anyway, we might not even be silverware for Brianna's party. We might surprise everyone with another idea."

"I want to be a spoon," Jessica said. "I'm sick of always being an astronaut or an alien. It's so obvious."

"Okay, I'll be the knife," Abby agreed. It solved her costume problem — finally!

"I wish you could come," Jessica said to Natalie.

"Besides, we need you," Abby added. "Without a fork, a knife and spoon can't eat anything besides pudding."

Natalie kicked at the fallen leaves covering the sidewalk. "I'll tell my parents that," she joked. "That'll convince them."

They reached Jessica's house. "Want to stay for a few minutes?" she asked.

They sat down on the porch steps. Jessica offered everyone a piece of a chocolate bar. They munched on chocolate and watched other kids walking home. Abby pulled out her journal.

If Brianna learns that Natalie's parents won't let her go, she will probably brag that she has the best parents in the fifth grade. Brianna can turn anything into a brag. How many years of hard work and sacrifice did it take her to develop this talent?

Will create special category in the <u>Hayes Book of World Records for Natalie</u>: Most Harry Potter Books Read by Fifth-Grader.

Will this be consolation for not going to party?

I don't think so.

Chapter 11

Saturday | morning

"Even if you're on the
right track, you'll get run
over if you just sit there."

—Will Rogers

No chance of me getting run over! My
baby-sitting day will not have much sitting
in it.

Plan E is the Plan to End All Plans.
Alex and I will have an Exciting, Energetic,
Eventful Day, which will persuade my parents what an Extremely Mature and Responsible Ten-Year-Old I am!

Everything will go well. My parents will
be elated. I will be exhausted, but who
cares, because next week is the festival!!!

Abby's mother pinned her keys to the waistband of her shorts. She pulled on a sweatshirt, picked up her water bottle, and said, for the hundredth time, "Now you know what to do, don't you, Abby?"

"Yes, Mom," Abby repeated. "If there's an emergency or if I have a question, I'll call the neighbors or Jessica's mom. I won't let anyone know that you and dad are gone, and I won't answer the door."

"Right," her mother said. "Take good care of Alex, lock up if you go out, and don't use the stove."

"Yes, Mom." Abby had baked the brownies this morning. Now all she had to do was add ice cream, whipped cream, and cherries. She would make the sundaes at the end of the afternoon. That way, she'd have a treat to promise Alex if he was good. Jessica had given her that baby-sitting tip.

"Now, Alex," her mother said, "you have to cooperate with Abby. Remember, she's in charge."

"Uh-huh."

"We'll have a great time, Alex!" Abby put her arm around him. "I've got a whole afternoon of exciting activities planned."

Her mother smiled. "Put on your jackets if you go to the park. Abby, you can make peanut butter and jelly sandwiches for lunch, can't you?"

"Mom, I'm an expert on peanut butter and jelly," Abby protested.

Their mother gave them each a quick hug. "Be good," she said.

"Win the race!" Abby said.

"Raise lots of money for those kids," Alex added.

Their mother checked her watch. "Got to run!" she said with a laugh. "I really do this time."

Abby locked the door behind her mother and turned to face her younger brother. "It's just the two of us now, Alex. What do you want to do first? Chess? Bike riding? Rollerblading? The park?"

"I want lunch." Alex watched Abby as if he wasn't sure of what she was going to do next. At least he wasn't whining that he wanted Eva or Isabel to baby-sit. "Then I want to go to the park. Then I want to play chess, then computer games."

"Anything," Abby promised him. Her heart was beating fast. She had played with Alex a million times, but this was different. This was the first time she was in charge and responsible.

Forty-five minutes later, she was pushing Alex on the swings in the park.

Alex had been quiet at first, but now he was having a good time. "Push me harder!" he yelled. "Higher!"

Abby pushed with all her strength. He soared out, then swung back. "I'm flying!" he called.

She pushed him again and again and again. Her arms were tired, but she wasn't complaining. So far everything was going well. She and Alex had eaten peanut butter and jelly sandwiches together, then cleaned up the kitchen. Afterward, they had walked to the park.

Until she decided to go to the festival with her friends, Alex always said that Abby was his favorite sister. She knew he felt hurt about her desertion.

Today she would make it all up to him. They would have an unforgettable day together.

"That was good," he said, when he got off. "What do we do next?"

"The jungle gym?"

"I love the jungle gym!" Alex grabbed her hand and began to run toward it. "Bet you can't hang upside down."

"Oh, yeah?" Abby said.

He shimmied up to the top and hung there like a koala bear. "Can you do this?" he demanded.

Abby hung from her knees. "Can you do this?"

"Yes!" Alex cried. He flipped upside down, then pulled himself up and sat on top of the bars. Abby followed him.

"I'm having fun," Alex said.

Abby smiled. Just wait until her parents heard about what a good time they had! Wait until they saw the clean kitchen! She had even wiped the counters. Wait until they saw what good care she had taken of Alex! The festival was a sure thing. Nothing could keep her from it now.

She jumped off the jungle gym. "Let's go down the slide," she yelled. "Race you over there. On your mark, get set, GO!"

Running across the grass, Abby let out a whoop. She was in good shape from the weeks of soccer practice and all the training she had done. "I'm going to beat you!" she cried. "I'm faster, stronger, and better!"

"No, you're not!" Alex yelled. "I am!"

He was gaining on her. For a second-grader who spent most of his time in front of the computer, he sure was fast. Then again, even at her best she wasn't that fast for a fifth-grader. Playing soccer had improved her speed, but not much.

Maybe Alex had inherited Isabel's mind *and* Eva's sports genes. Thank goodness he was younger. An older SuperSib genius sports star was the last thing Abby needed.

"Can't stop me!" Alex sprinted past her, waving his arms.

"Nyah, nyah, I'll catch up!"

Alex ran even faster, turning to see whether Abby was gaining on him.

"I'm going to get you!" Abby yelled, putting on a burst of speed.

"No! Never!" Alex cried. With a wild whoop, he leaped forward and crashed straight into the slide.

At first Abby thought it was just a bump. Alex had gotten hundreds of them.

Then he turned toward her, cupping his face in his hands. Blood poured out between his fingers.

Abby's heart pounded. There was blood everywhere. She raced toward him. "Are you okay?" she cried. "Are you okay, Alex?"

He clutched his forehead. "No!" he shrieked. "No!"

She pulled off her scarf and pressed it against his head. In a moment, the scarf was soaked.

"I want Mom!" he cried.

"Okay, we'll get her. You're going to be all right," Abby said. It had to be true. She hoped it was true. "We'll get Mom," she repeated. She didn't know where. Right now her mother was thirty miles out of town and running a marathon around a lake.

Frantically, she looked for an adult. There was no one in sight, only a few kids on the swings.

She felt dizzy with fear. Where was the phone? Should she call an ambulance? She tried to remember what she had learned in summer camp about injuries. If it was an artery — but there weren't any arteries in the forehead. Could he faint from loss of blood? Could he die? There was so much blood!

Jessica . . . Her house was only a block away. Her mother was home. She would help them.

"Can you walk?" she asked Alex. Her voice was shaking.

In answer, he howled even more loudly. "Mom! Mom!"

She grabbed his arm and pulled him toward the street. She couldn't leave him here alone. She had to get him help.

"We're going to get Jessica's mom," she said loudly. "She'll know what to do."

A few minutes later, the two of them stumbled onto Jessica's porch. Blood trailed behind them on the sidewalk and stairs. Abby pressed the doorbell as hard as she could.

"What — " Jessica's mother began as she opened the door.

Abby pointed to her brother and burst into tears.

Jessica's mother took one look at Alex and grabbed her car keys from the stand by the door. "Jessica!" she yelled.

"Get in the car," she ordered Alex and Abby. "We're going to the emergency room."

In the car, Abby held Alex's hand. If he was okay, she thought, she would never get mad at him again, even if he won seventy games of chess in a row. She would go to the festival with him and do everything he wanted to do. She would never complain again about him wanting to do everything with her and Jessica.

She had let him down in the park. She shouldn't have raced him. She shouldn't have tried to beat him. If he was okay, she would let him win everything for the rest of his life.

"I'm sorry, Alex," she whispered. "I'm really sorry."

Chapter 12

Saturday evening

"Experience is the name everyone gives to their mistakes."

—Mark Twain

Wooden Raft Calendar

Boy, do I have a lot of experience! Too much, if you ask me:

Number of stitches Alex had to have in the emergency room: 14

Number of times I said, "It's all my fault!" 500 per minute

Number of times Jessica's mom tried to reassure me it wasn't: about the same

Number of times I believed her: 0

Number of ice-cream scoops eaten by Alex Hayes after his stitches: 3 large ones

Number of ice-cream scoops eaten by Abby Hayes: 0

(Note: This is the first time in recorded history that I have ever refused ice cream. But my stomach was so wobbly that I thought I was going to throw up.)

E is for Emergency. Why didn't I know that? F is for Failure and Forget about the Festival.

Missing the festival is the least of my problems! My parents will never trust me again! I will be lucky if they let me walk to school on my own! Or ride my bike around the block!

Maybe I am a Menace to Humanity. In the interests of public safety, I should stay in my room for the rest of my life.

At least Alex is going to be okay. (HOORAY!!!!) He has luckily survived what will probably be the only baby-sitting job I ever have.

When we got home, I made him change his clothes and put the dirty ones in the wash. My scarf is ruined, but who cares?

＊　＊　＊

My mother is not home yet. Jessica and her mom are in the living room, playing board games with Alex. They are staying with us until my mother gets here.

I said, "I know. You don't trust me with Alex. I don't blame you."

Jessica's mom said, "Not at all, Abby! You're too upset to be left alone. I wouldn't want to be alone after taking my little brother to the emergency room."

 New category for the <u>Hayes Book of World Records</u>: Nicest Person to Have Around in an Emergency. Jessica's mom.

What is my mother going to do when she walks in?

What I think will happen:

1. My mother will faint.

2. My mother will yell, cry, and shriek.

3. My mother will take away all my privileges for the rest of my life. She and my father will put me on a diet of bread and water. I will live alone in my prison

cell of a room, with only calendars to console me and mark the time.

What will probably happen:
1. My mother will be very disappointed in me.
2. My mother will be extremely angry at me.
3. I will be grounded for two weeks.
4. I will miss the festival and Brianna's birthday party.

Do you think I care about missing the festival or Brianna's party? NO! All those worries have been sucked out of me, as if a vacuum cleaner came and scooped out my insides.

I hear a car. It might be my mother.
It is my mother. . . .

I wish I had wings and could fly away.
I wish I had a cloak of invisibility and could disappear.

I wish I had the power to change shapes and could become a dog or a hamster for a few hours until my mother calms down.

I wish I were part of a fairy tale, so this would end happily ever after.

Abby's mother came into the house. Alex, Jessica, and her mom were in the living room.

"Where's Abby?" her mother cried. "Is she okay? I had a feeling something was wrong!"

Jessica's mom pointed to Alex's forehead. "He had an accident," she said. "We took him to the emergency room. He needed a few stitches, but he's fine now."

"Abby!" her mother called.

Abby came in slowly from behind the door.

Her mother had pulled Alex onto her lap. Jessica's mom and Jessica were on the floor in front of a board game. They weren't really playing, though.

"There you are, Abby," her mother said. She didn't sound too angry. "I'm glad to see you. Tell me what happened."

Abby gave her all the details. Then she waited for the worst.

I'm still so astonished, I can hardly write it down. My mother thanked me for having a cool head in an emergency.

(The cool head felt like a bunch of eggs getting scrambled.)

She said I had done exactly the right thing.

"But it was my fault!" I burst out. "If I hadn't been racing Alex, he wouldn't have hit his head on the slide!"

"How often have you raced Alex?" my mother asked quietly.

My face was hot. I didn't answer.

"Millions of times, I bet," my mother said.

"Yeah, I guess so."

"And how many times has he run into a slide?"

"Just once," I admitted.

"So you couldn't have known he would hit his head if you raced him," my mother concluded with a flourish.

I see why my mother is a successful lawyer. Unstoppable logic
and good interrogation techniques.

She said she was glad everyone
was okay. She said going to Jessica's house was exactly the right
thing to do and that I had
shown good sense. She said most kids got
stitches at one time or another in their
lives, and she hoped Alex had gotten them
over with.

(Are stitches like chicken pox? I don't
think so.)

"The doctor said I was the bravest
seven-year-old she had ever seen!" Alex
bragged.

Was glad to hear seven-year-old brother
bragging. Not obnoxious as it is with
Brianna. A sign of health and happiness.

"I used to jump off tables when I was
four," my mother told us. "I broke my arm
once and my leg twice. I had to get
stitches when I crashed through the back
door."

My mom invited Jessica and her mom to stay for dinner. We made spaghetti and salad and had brownies with ice cream (again!) for dessert. This time I ate everything.

Is this a fairy tale? The ending is "happily ever after." At least I think so. So much has happened today that I am exhausted. I want to sleep for a long time.

P.S. Alex and I did have an unforgettable afternoon together!

Chapter 13

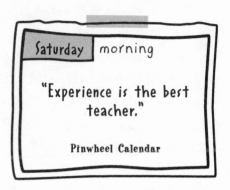

Saturday morning

"Experience is the best
teacher."

Pinwheel Calendar

I prefer Ms. Bunder to be my teacher!
Or Ms. Kantor, or one of my parents, or
even one of my SuperSisters!

Things I learned from Alex's accident:
The sight of blood makes me feel sick.
Don't race in parks without an adult
around.
Always remind Alex to watch where he's
going.
Parents are unpredictable. They get angry
when you forget to take colored markers out

of your jeans pockets before putting them in the wash and other dumb things like that.

When it comes to something really important, though, like accidents and blood and stitches, they're understanding and calm. (Does this happen all the time with everyone's parents? Or was I just lucky? I don't want to test this idea out!)

TODAY IS THE FESTIVAL! I CAN BIKE THERE WITH JESSICA! I HAVE EIGHT DOLLARS TO SPEND! HOORAY!

This is a very exciting weekend. First the festival and then, tomorrow morning, Jessica and I are going to do our costumes for Brianna's party. Natalie is going to help us. Then she will go home where she will be suddenly stricken by Spotted Newt Fever or Mongoose Pox or Purple Lightning Madness, which will force her to cancel her appearance as a fork at Brianna's Best Birthday Bash.

"There will be a tall, dark stranger in your life," Isabel predicted to Abby in the hallway of the Hayes house. She was dressed as a fortune-teller in a silver vest, worn over a red embroidered blouse and a long velvet skirt. She had put on gold earrings, lots of makeup, and for the occasion had newly painted her fingernails to match her blouse.

"When?" Abby said.

The doorbell rang. Alex ran to open the door. "It's Jessica!" he cried. "She's on her bike! It's time to leave for the festival!"

"My prediction has come true," Isabel said in her most mysterious voice.

"Jessica's tall and dark, but not a stranger," Abby joked.

"Two out of three isn't bad," Isabel said. "I bet most fortune-tellers don't get it right that often."

Jessica wiped her feet on the mat. She was wearing boot-leg jeans and a heavy fleece sweater. Her gloves and socks were rainbow-striped. Her bike helmet dangled over her arm. "I like your costume, Isabel!"

Isabel took Jessica's hand. "For your kind words, I will read your fortune for free." She traced her finger over the knitted fabric of Jessica's glove. "I see red. . . . I see blue. . . . You will lead a very colorful life," she concluded.

"Gee," Jessica said. "What if I had worn my white mittens?"

Abby tied the laces of her sneakers into multiple knots so they wouldn't catch in the gearshift of her bike. She checked her pockets to make sure she had her money. Then she picked up her bike helmet and adjusted the straps.

"Have you got your stitches out yet?" Jessica asked Alex.

"Yep." He pointed to his forehead.

"That's some scar," Jessica said admiringly.

"Everyone in second grade is jealous." Abby fastened the strap of her helmet. "No one else at Lancaster Elementary has a mean-looking scar like that."

Alex struck a karate pose. "I got it in a laser fight with the forces of darkness!"

"The evil Slide Master got you," Abby said, grabbing him in a hug.

"Good-bye," her father said, giving her a kiss at the door. "I'm really proud of you, Abby."

"For what?"

"For inviting Alex to bike with you and Jessica to the festival. That shows a lot of maturity."

"Really?" I said.

"Yes," her father said. "You're growing up."

Abby's mother nodded her head.

"We'll be there in half an hour or so. Ride safely, especially when you cross the street."

"Of course, Mom!" Abby promised. "We'll be very careful."

"We know you will," her parents said.

Abby turned to her little brother. "Ready, Alex?"

"Yes!" Alex said. He tightened his helmet strap, then reached into his pocket and pulled out a five-dollar bill. "Look how much I got to spend!"

"That should be enough to stuff yourself with cotton candy," Abby observed.

The three of them got on their bikes.

"Don't worry, Mom and Dad, we won't let him ride into any slides!" They pedaled down the street toward the high school.

The first thing Abby, Jessica, and Alex saw when they entered the high school gymnasium was a six-year-old girl throwing wet sponges at the gym teacher, Mr. Stevens, who stood behind a screen with only his head showing.

He wasn't too wet, at least not yet. Zach and Tyler were standing in line with their tickets. "We're going to get him soaked," they promised.

"Okay, hit me with your best shot!" Mr. Stevens encouraged the girl.

"My dad did that last year," Abby said. "He got really drenched."

"Smart guy," Mr. Stevens commented, "not to do it again this year."

They passed a table of brownies, cakes, and muffins for sale, then another where kids were making candy-coated apples.

"There's Natalie!" Alex yelled.

She sat at the face-painting booth, having her face decorated with green leaves.

"Nice foliage," Abby said.

"Thanks!" Natalie peered into the mirror at the green leaves trailing over her face. "Isn't this fun?"

"I want flames on my face," Jessica announced.

"We can do that." It was Bethany's mother. She didn't look anything like Bethany, except the shape of her eyes. She was wearing jeans and a sweatshirt and sneakers, not the kind of clothes that Bethany wore.

Bethany's mom picked up a paintbrush, dabbed it

in orange-red paint, and began to draw flames going up Jessica's cheeks. "How about you? Do you want flames, too?" she asked Abby. "Or do you want leaves? I can do butterflies or cats or rainbows, too."

"I definitely don't want flames," Abby said. "My hair already looks like it's on fire!"

Alex tugged at Abby's hand. "I want to be a robot," he said.

"You're next," Bethany's mom promised him. "I have lots of silver makeup waiting just for you."

He sat down. She smoothed silver face paint expertly over his skin, then gave him large square eyes, a straight red mouth, and a green nose.

"Hey, Alex!" It was Eva. There was a bag of brightly colored balls slung over her shoulder. "Ready to come with me?"

"I — am — a — robot," Alex said in a mechanical voice. "I — am — dangerous."

He gave Abby a quick hug and then took Eva's hand. "Take — me — to — your — leader."

With a wave, they disappeared into the crowd.

It was Abby's turn to have her face painted. "Can you put smile faces all over my face?" she asked Bethany's mom. "That way, even if I don't feel like smiling, I'll still look friendly," she explained to her friends.

As Bethany's mom put the last smile on the last round yellow circle, Paul Hayes appeared with his video camera. "Let me get a shot of you, girls!" he said. "You look great!"

Natalie, Jessica, and Abby put their arms around each other and mugged for the camera.

"Terrific!" Abby's father said. He lowered the camera. "Did Eva take Alex?"

"They left a few minutes ago," Abby said.

Her father picked up his camera again as a group of kids in animal masks passed by. "Well, enjoy yourselves, girls! You're on your own now."

The three girls hugged each other again.

"We're on our own now!" Abby repeated. "Yes!"

Saturday night.

Number of predictions Isabel made at the festival: 357

Number that have come true: 0

Number of predictions that Isabel says will come true: all of them (If so, she will get a category in the

Hayes Book of World Records.)

Number of times Zach and Tyler hit Mr. Stevens with a sponge: 5

Number of sit-ups he has threatened to make them do next week in gym class: 700 (Ha-ha. I think he's joking.)

Amount of fun we had: A LOT!!!

Natalie even said the festival almost made up for not being able to go to Brianna's party tomorrow.

Chapter 14

Sunday

"Friendship is the finest flower in the garden of life."

Marigold Calendar

Is friendship a flower? If so, Jessica would start wheezing every time she saw me. She is allergic to most flowers!

Yesterday was the festival; today is Brianna's birthday party. This weekend is an embarrassment of riches, as Isabel likes to say.

I wonder why riches are an embarrassment. A happiness of riches or a joy of riches is more like it.

"Here we are," Abby's mother said as she pulled up to Brianna's house. It was big and white, with a landscaped yard. "Have a good time at the party."

Jessica and Abby got out of the car. Abby was wearing dark pants for the butter knife handle. She had made the blade from cardboard and taped it on with duct tape. Jessica was dressed all in gray. She had a round spoon top. Both girls had painted their faces silver. They were carrying brightly wrapped presents.

"I got Brianna a ballet dancer calendar," Abby said as they walked up to the door. "What did you get?"

"My mom and I bought her a mirror and hair-brush set."

"A mirror — that's the perfect gift for Brianna," Abby agreed.

They rang the bell. The door swung open.

"Welcome to Brianna's birthday party!" Brianna greeted them. She was dressed in a green satin gown with large pink brocade flowers and a long velvet sash. On her head she wore a tiara of fake diamonds.

"Ooooh, presents! I love presents!" she squealed.

"They're for you," Abby said. "Happy birthday."

Brianna took the presents. "I'm so sorry about Natalie," she said. "It's such a shame."

"Yes," Abby and Jessica chorused.

"I hope she didn't spread it to everyone yesterday at the festival," Bethany said. She was dressed as a mouse in white fur, with a hood and pink ears.

"No," they said together.

"Pinkeye is such a contagious disease," Brianna said. "I've never had it!"

"She got medicine," Abby said. "You know, those antibiotic eyedrops. They work really fast. She'll be better tomorrow."

In the next room, someone banged a drum. A clarinet squawked. Someone turned up an amplifier, then turned it down again.

"You got here just in time for the music. Come on!" Brianna waved Abby and Jessica into the living room.

Crepe paper spirals crisscrossed the room; shiny balloons hung everywhere; winking lights outlined the ceiling and windows. At one end of the room was a long table piled with food: pizza cut into tiny triangles, miniature hot dogs, bowls of popcorn, candy kisses, fruit punch, five different kinds of soda, and platters of grapes and strawberries.

Almost the entire class was there. Everyone was in

costume. There were fairies, dancers, pirates, ghosts, and a few cartoon characters. There was also a cat, a mailbox, a computer Web site, and a giant grape.

The band began to play.

"Want a kiss?" Brianna held up a silver-wrapped candy to Zach.

"Uh, no thanks." Zach had white hair and a suit jacket and was bent over a cane.

"You're sure? Not even for the birthday girl?"

He shook his head. A shower of white powder fell on his shoulders. "Look. Dandruff. I put flour in my hair to make it white."

"That's disgusting, Zach." Brianna unwrapped the kiss and popped it into her own mouth. "I hope you don't get flour all over the living room! It'll make my mom crazy."

Brianna's mom carried a bowl of potato chips to the food table. She was wearing a tight, short skirt and a bright blue jacket. Her hair was short and styled. Her lipstick was red; her high heels matched her jacket.

"She looks like a model, not a mom," Abby whispered to Jessica.

"Having fun at our little party?" Brianna's mom asked Tyler, who was wearing an ape suit.

He swung his arms and hiccuped. "Sure," he said.

"Let's dance!" Brianna cried.

No one moved.

Brianna put her hands on her hips. "Doesn't anyone want to dance?"

"You go first, Brianna," her mother encouraged her. "After all, you've been dancing since you were two years old."

Brianna waved her arms gracefully and then began to do a complicated dance step across the floor. "Come on, everyone! Zach, dance with me!"

"I'm too old," he croaked.

After a few minutes, Bethany hip-hopped out onto the floor in her white mouse costume to join her best friend. Tyler swung his arms wildly and leaped in front of her.

Pretty soon everyone was dancing. Even Zach threw away his cane and joined in.

"Isn't this the best party ever?" Brianna yelled.

"Yay, Brianna!" Bethany called. "You're the best!"

Sunday night.
Brianna's party was good! Dancing in costumes was a lot of fun. Some people couldn't move too well, like the grape and

the mailbox (Meghan and Rachel), while others, like Zach and Tyler, danced in character. Tyler made a lot of ape motions and
noises, which was pretty obnoxious, while
Zach pretended that his bones were aching,
which was funny. Jessica and I made up
a knife-and-spoon dance.

When we were done dancing, Brianna's
mom brought out the birthday cake. It was
a vanilla layer cake deco-
rated with a picture of a
ballerina and a soccer goal
in the background and said,
in pink icing: "Happy birthday,
Brianna! Always strive to be the best!"

We all got miniature soccer balls to take
home. Also a bag of sparkly pencils, erasers,
and candies.

When we got home, Jessica and I called
Natalie. Her parents took her to Paradise
Pizza for lunch. She wore dark glasses so
no one could see her eyes. Tomorrow she
will wear them to school. Jessica saved a
piece of cake for her. I offered to give her
my party favors.

Everyone in my family was in a good mood tonight. Even me.

I kept the silver paint on my face and pretended to be a robot to make Alex laugh. Eva and Isabel did not fight at the table. An unprecedented period of world peace. I wonder how long it will last. (Uh-oh. I hear screaming down the hall. The truce has already been broken.)

While we were clearing the table after dinner, my father told me that I have been very mature lately.

So there! I'm mature! I knew it all along! I'm glad my parents have finally caught on.

Will they let me get pierced ears now? Must ask soon. Seize the moment. Grab the second. Arm wrestle the quarter hour.

Earrings are the final frontier. If I could have pierced ears, I would have EVERY-THING I want. Well, almost everything.

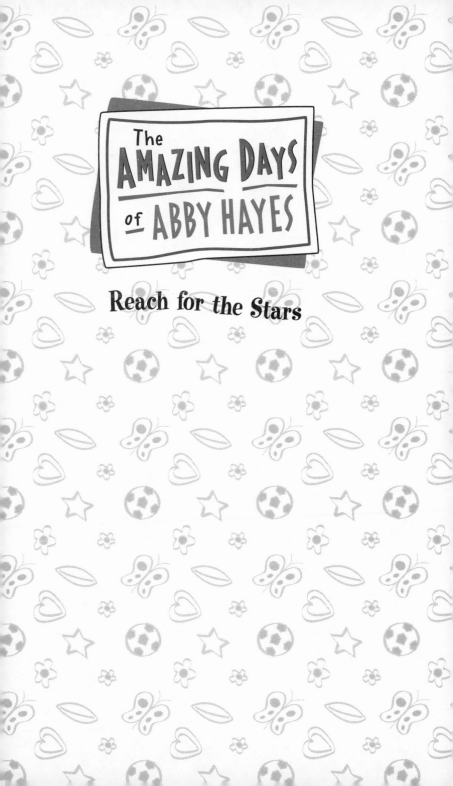

The AMAZING DAYS of ABBY HAYES

Reach for the Stars

For Helen,

Purple pens forever!

Chapter 1

Thursday

"The play's the thing."
—William Shakespeare

Tropical Fruit Calendar

Hooray! It really <u>is</u> the thing! Ms. Bunder and Ms. Kantor announced today that our class is going to put on a production of <u>Peter Pan</u> for the entire school. We will paint the sets, design the costumes, and, of course, act in the play! Everyone in Ms. Kantor's fifth grade will have something to do. I hope I will have a <u>lot</u> to do!

Abby Hayes, her best friend, Jessica, and their new friend, Natalie, sat in the school cafeteria. They pushed aside their trays and lunch boxes and cleared a space on the table.

"Okay, let's figure this out." Jessica pulled a pen from her overalls pocket, wiped an invisible speck of lint from the sleeve of her pale-blue sweater, and wrote "*Peter Pan*" at the top of a piece of paper.

Abby's best friend was always organized and neat. If you were looking for a ruler, an eraser, or a piece of paper, Jessica was the first person to ask.

"Yes, let's write down the roles," Abby said. She pushed an unruly lock of curly red hair from her face and peered at the blank piece of paper. "The tryouts are in two weeks. Let's figure out who wants to try out for which role."

Natalie nodded in agreement. "Then we can practice together." She was small and slim with short dark hair. Her blue sweatshirt had mysterious green stains on it. They were probably from the chemistry experiments she liked to do at home.

Jessica chewed on the end of her pen. Her asthma inhaler poked out of her overalls pocket. "There are a lot of great roles in *Peter Pan*," she said. "There's Wendy, Tinkerbell, Peter Pan . . ."

"That's who I want to be!" Abby interrupted.

"Can you fly?" Natalie teased her.

"I'll learn!" Abby said. "Ms. Bunder says you can learn anything if you try hard enough." Ms. Bunder was Abby's favorite teacher. She came to Ms. Kantor's class once a week to teach creative writing.

"I want to be John or Michael," Natalie said, "one of Wendy's little brothers. Do you think I could pass as a boy?"

Abby and Jessica studied her for a moment.

"If you combed your hair differently," Jessica said.

"If you put on boy's clothes," Abby said, "it'd be easy. I'd do it in a minute for the right role."

Natalie slicked her hair back. "There!" she said. She strutted back and forth in front of the table. "Now do I look like a boy?"

"Maybe *you* should be Peter Pan," Abby said. "Then you can fly just like Harry Potter does."

Natalie loved the Harry Potter books. She had read each one fourteen times and was working on her fifteenth round. "Maybe. But don't you want to try out for Peter Pan, Abby?"

Abby shrugged. "Either Peter Pan or Captain Hook." She waved her arms menacingly and scowled at her friends. "Captain Hook would be fun. Then again, maybe I should be Wendy."

Jessica pointed to the paper. "Let's get this all down." She began to write. "There's Smee, the Lost Boys, the Crocodile, Nana . . ."

"Jessica, you should be Tinkerbell," Abby said.

"No!" Jessica protested. "I want a quick walk-on part. You can be Peter Pan or Wendy, I'll be happy to be a pirate."

"Did I hear someone say 'Wendy'?" It was Brianna, the first girl in the fifth grade to wear matching nail polish and colored lip gloss. As usual, she was dressed as if she were about to walk down a runway. In spite of the chilly weather outside, she had on a cap-sleeved short black dress with chunky-heeled, bump-toed shoes. Her arms were bare, but that didn't seem to bother Brianna as long as she could wear the most fashionable clothes.

"We're deciding which roles to audition for," Abby told her.

Brianna smiled. "I've had the lead in every play I've been in since kindergarten. The role of Wendy is *mine*."

"If you're Wendy, I'm Tinkerbell." Her best friend, Bethany, giggled. Bethany wore a fleece jumper with a long-sleeved red shirt underneath. Her hair was long and blond instead of long and dark, like Brianna's. Other than that, it was hard to tell the two of them apart. "What a team we'll be."

"Ms. Bunder is going to decide," Abby reminded

them. "We all have to try out for the parts we want."

"I've auditioned all my life," Brianna announced with a flounce of her head. "I take ballet lessons and dance with the Hot Shots. I study voice, drama, and French. *Oui? Oui? N'est-ce pas?* Yes, yes, isn't that right?" she translated as her classmates stared at her in confusion.

Not only could Brianna speak French, sing, dance, and act, but she was the biggest bragger in the fifth grade. When it came to bragging, no one could keep up with her.

"Yay, Brianna," Bethany cheered.

"The role of Wendy was made for me," Brianna continued. "Or maybe I was made for the role of Wendy."

Abby exchanged glances with her friends. Brianna had been starring in plays since before she was born. If she wanted to be Wendy, Abby would be crazy to even try for the role. Still . . .

"Everyone will have a chance," Abby said, quoting Ms. Bunder.

"No one will have a chance next to me," Brianna retorted. "No one in fifth grade has the experience and knowledge that I do."

"Yay, Brianna," Bethany said again.

The two best friends linked arms and walked away.

"Weee, weeee, weee," Natalie said, imitating Brianna's French. "Isn't that what the fifth little piggy said all the way home?"

"We can't let Brianna annoy us," Abby said. She was speaking to herself as much as to Natalie and Jessica. "How much do experience and knowledge count, anyway? Maybe we're naturally talented."

"I don't think so," Jessica said. "I forgot my lines when I was a potato in my kindergarten play. It's all been downhill from there."

"I've never really been in a play," Natalie said. "This is so exciting."

"I've been in some skits," Abby said, "but this is my first time in a real play, too." Like Natalie, she found it very exciting. She hoped she could learn what she needed along the way. Not only did she want to do everything — act, paint, and help with costumes — but she wanted to do everything well.

This was a chance to show Ms. Bunder that she was good at more than just writing. Wouldn't Ms. Bunder be thrilled when she discovered all of Abby's talents!

"The idea of being onstage for more than a few

minutes makes me nervous," Jessica confessed. "I want to work mostly on the scenery and costumes."

"Not me!" Abby exclaimed. "I can't wait to be onstage!" She could already see herself. She would dance gracefully and sing like a bird. She would make the audience laugh and weep. Her SuperSibs would beg for her autograph.

"Is Brianna really that good?" Natalie asked. Her family had moved to town only a few months before, and she was still getting to know everyone. "Or does she just think she is?"

"She *is* a really good dancer," Abby admitted. "She's been in a lot of plays, too."

Jessica pulled her inhaler from her pocket and took a puff. "Don't worry, I bet you can learn your lines better than she can."

"We will!" Natalie and Abby said.

"Are you talking about the play?" Zach and Tyler came over and sat down next to the three friends.

"Yes!" the girls chorused.

"I'm going to be Captain Hook!" Zach announced. "With a computer-generated arm! I'm going to have it light up and make computer sounds."

Zach and Tyler were the resident fifth-grade computer fanatics — or gamies, as Abby called them. They spent most of their spare time in front of small square blinking screens.

"Smee," Tyler said. "Smee is me. Don't you think so?"

"Definitely," Abby agreed.

She wasn't going to tell Zach and Tyler that she was thinking of trying out for Captain Hook, too. They would just laugh at her. But why shouldn't she? If Peter Pan had always been played by girls or women, why not Captain Hook? All she had to do was pin up her wild red hair and hide it under a pirate's hat. She'd wear a black eye patch and a sailor's shirt. Tonight, as soon as she got home, she'd go up to her room and start practicing an evil laugh.

"The tryouts are in two weeks," Zach said, "and the play is in two months. That's not a lot of time. Especially if we're going to put it on for the whole school and our families."

This was another reason Abby wanted to shine in the play. Her family was good at *everything*. Her twin ninth-grade sisters, Eva and Isabel, were Super-Muscled and SuperBrained. Her younger brother, Alex, was in second grade and already a computer genius and a math whiz. Her father ran his own business, setting up his clients to do business on the Internet. Her mother was a successful lawyer. The Hayeses were not Type A's — they were Type A pluses!

Sometimes Abby wondered if she had been beamed in from another planet. She was *so* different from the rest of the amazing Hayes family. She wasn't a genius, a superstar, or even a highly successful person. She was an ordinary fifth-grader (with flaming red hair) who loved to write in her journal and collect calendars.

If she was a star in the play, she might prove, once and for all, that she really belonged in her family. Besides, neither of her older sisters had ever starred in a play. Abby would be the first Hayes to shine onstage.

The bell rang. Abby, Jessica, and Natalie gathered up their trays and lunch boxes and headed back to Ms. Kantor's room.

Chapter 2

Friday

"A thing of beauty is a joy forever."

— *John Keats*

Striped Socks Calendar

My performance in <u>Peter Pan</u> will be a "thing of beauty." It will be a "joy forever," because my family will never stop talking about it. Neither will Ms. Bunder. The tryouts are in only two weeks. I must prepare myself in every way. Once I get my part, I will rehearse without cease!

But first I must decide which part I want. Captain Hook? Peter Pan? Wendy? Or any of the other roles?

Pluses and Minuses:

WENDY.

PLUS: A starring role. Get to be wise older sister and best friend of Peter Pan.

MINUS: Must compete with Brianna for the role. (She will be nasty if she doesn't get the part, and even worse if she does.)

TINKERBELL.

PLUS: Another starring role. No lines to memorize.

MINUS: Can't stand the name! Don't want to be a cute little fairy with wings!

MICHAEL OR JOHN.

PLUS: Get to sing, dance, and be on-stage.

MINUS: Don't want to spend the entire play in boys' pajamas.

PETER PAN.

PLUS: The best part in the play. Sings and dances and never has to grow up. Wears cute elf costume.

MINUS: What are the chances of my getting it?

CAPTAIN HOOK.

PLUS: Gets to wave mean-looking hook and menace everyone. Sword fight with Peter Pan.

MINUS: Will the boys laugh at me for trying out for this role?

When Abby came home from school on Friday, there was a letter waiting for her on the hall table. It was in a long, shiny envelope with pictures of cats all over the front and back. Her name and address were printed on a small white label. She recognized the thin black lettering right away.

"It's from Grandma Emma!" she called. Grandma Emma, her mother's mother, was her favorite relative. She lived halfway across the country with her dog, Zipper.

Abby wanted to tear the envelope open, but she didn't. Grandma Emma's envelopes were all handmade from catalog pages or old magazines. Abby saved them in a large manila folder. Grandma Emma had promised that the next time she came to visit, she would teach Abby to make her own envelopes.

She yanked open the drawer where her mother kept a letter opener, then carefully slit the envelope open. Grandma Emma's favorite stationery slid out.

Abby scanned the letter quickly and then yelled to Alex. "Grandma Emma is coming to visit!"

"Hooray!" he yelled back.

She ran to her room to check the dates on a calendar.

There were plenty of calendars to check. Abby had seventy-four. She had been collecting them since first grade. There was the Spuds Calendar she bought in fourth grade, the Polar Bear Calendar she slept with in first grade, and the Ancient Monuments Calendar her third-grade teacher had given her. Her newest calendars were the World Cup Soccer Calendar she had bought when she was trying out for the soccer team and the Genius Calendar Natalie had given her a month ago. Those were the ones she kept dates on.

She flipped through the pages of the Genius Calendar with its pictures of Einstein, Shakespeare, and Mozart. Maybe one day her sister Isabel would have her face on a Genius Calendar. Or her little brother, Alex. Eva was more likely to show up on a sports calendar. She was the captain of her lacrosse, basketball, and swim teams.

Abby marked the date of her grandmother's arrival in purple. There was another purple date circled the same week: the play! Wait until Grandma Emma heard! She would get to visit the Hayes family *and* see Abby perform.

Grandma Emma and Abby had a special relationship. When Abby was a baby, Grandma Emma had taken care of her every day. Plus, there was the red hair. When she was younger, Grandma Emma had wild, curly hair just like Abby's, though now it was white. She didn't collect calendars, but she had hundreds of salt and pepper shakers in her house. They were in the shapes of animals, people, and national monuments.

Abby unzipped her backpack and searched for the script. Now she was going to get to work! Grandma Emma would be in the audience the night of her performance. She began to read the play out loud, putting lots of expression into her voice.

Just as Peter Pan was about to confront Captain Hook, Abby's bedroom door flew open.

"Abby, have you seen my science notebook? I can't find it anywhere!"

It was her SuperSister Isabel, top student in her grade, winner of history awards, and school representative to a national debate in Washington, D.C., in a few months. Aside from being a straight-A student, Isabel loved clothes and fingernail polish. Today she wore a short suede skirt and a black Lycra top. Her nails were painted dark red to match her skirt.

"Haven't seen it," Abby said. She pointed to her writing notebook. "This is the only one I have. What about Eva?"

"Eva?" Isabel said. She stamped her foot. "Eva!"

"Did someone call me?" Abby's other SuperSister poked her head in the door. Unlike her more fashionable twin, she wore jeans and a T-shirt. Her hair was pulled away from her face with a sweatband. She was carrying a gym bag in one hand and a towel in the other.

"What did you do with my science notebook?" Isabel demanded.

"I haven't touched your science notebook! Why would I?"

"Because you were at the gym last night instead of studying for the test tomorrow! My notes are better than yours, and you know it!"

"For your information, I studied an hour last night from my own notes," Eva snapped. "Thank goodness I'm not an oversized brain in a glass jar!"

"At least I can think for myself!" Isabel retorted. "It's better than spending all my time trying to put a ridiculous ball through a little hoop!"

"Ridiculous? *You're* calling *basketball* ridiculous?"

The twins were like positive and negative charges. Put them together and you had an automatic explosion.

Abby held up the script. "I'm trying to do some schoolwork," she announced. "Could you go somewhere else?"

"I'm not leaving until I find my notebook!" Isabel exclaimed.

"I'm not leaving until Isabel apologizes!" Eva cried.

Abby sighed. Maybe she should go hide in the closet. Or lock herself in the bathroom. Or find a new family. One without twin SuperSisters who fought.

"Can someone make me hot chocolate?" It was Alex, their younger brother. He had a faint scar over his left eyebrow, where he had run into a slide. His hair was tousled and messy. His sweatshirt was on backward. At least his socks matched. That was better than usual.

"I will!" Abby jumped up, eager to be away from her older sisters. She picked up the script of *Peter Pan*. Maybe Alex would help her rehearse.

"Have you seen my science notebook, Alex?" Isabel asked.

Alex ran his fingers through his already messy hair. "It's in the kitchen," he said. "I was reading it."

"My science notebook?"

He nodded.

Abby held her breath and waited for the explosion. Isabel was very particular about her belongings.

"You were reading my honors science notes?" Isabel said again.

"Uh-huh."

Isabel beamed at her younger brother. "If you have any questions, just ask me. And next time, put it back in my room when you're done, okay?"

Abby stared at her older sister in amazement. Isabel wasn't mad at Alex for taking her notebook. Instead she seemed proud of him. If it had been Eva who had taken it, she would have blasted her with full nuclear power.

"You owe me two apologies now," Eva snapped.

"Do I?" Isabel retorted. "I don't think so."

Abby grabbed Alex's arm. "Come on, Alex! Time to make hot chocolate."

As they went down the stairs, Alex asked, "Why do they fight so much?"

"I don't know," Abby said. "It's just the way they are." It wasn't a good explanation, but it was the only one she had.

"In *Peter Pan*, the two brothers, John and Michael, don't fight at all," Abby told him. "Can you believe that?"

"No," Alex said.

"It's easier to believe in Tinkerbell and Peter Pan than in two siblings who never fight," Abby observed.

Alex grabbed her hand. "I'm glad *we* don't fight, Abby."

"Oh, sometimes we do," she said. "Just not as much as the twins."

It was hard to keep up with Eva and Isabel when it came to fighting. They probably broke a world record for it every day. She'd have to remember to put them in the *Hayes Book of World Records*. Eva and Isabel ought to win in the Frequent Fight category as well as Most Creative Insults and Most Fights with Fewest Reasons.

In the kitchen, their father was putting a roast into the oven. Abby's father worked at home in a converted attic office. Their mother worked in a big law firm and was often home late. She and their father divided up most of the household chores. Their father cooked, got the kids off to school in the morning, and shopped. Their mother did laundry and supervised the cleaning. Abby, Alex, Isabel, and Eva all helped out.

"Guess who's coming to visit?" her father asked.

Abby closed her eyes and waved her hands in the air. "I am getting an answer. . . ." she intoned. "With my psychic powers I will divine the truth. The answer is . . ."

"Grandma Emma!" Alex blurted.

Her father shook his head. "I thought I was going to surprise you two. I should have known better."

"She wrote me a letter," Abby explained. "I told Alex."

"Is she bringing Zipper?" Alex asked. He loved animals, but the Hayes family couldn't have any because of his allergies.

"No, she has to leave him in a kennel with his friends," their father said.

Alex looked disappointed.

"Guess what, Dad?" Abby said.

"I don't have your psychic powers," her father joked. "You better just tell me."

Abby waved her script at her father. "I'm going to be in a play, and it's the same week Grandma Emma is here!"

Her father pulled out the chopping board and knife and began to slice onions. "I'm sure she'll be thrilled."

"It's *Peter Pan*! I want to be Peter Pan or Captain Hook. Or maybe Wendy, if Brianna doesn't get the part."

"You'll be good at whatever you choose," her father said encouragingly.

"Dad! That's what you always say!"

"Be Peter Pan," Alex said. "He dances a lot. I saw the movie."

"Dad, can I take dance lessons?" Abby asked.

Her father smiled. "Why don't you get the part first, and then we'll talk about it."

Abby sighed. It was just like her parents to wait for results first. Didn't they know she had to start preparing *now*? She had to catch up with Brianna, who had been doing this all her life. Two weeks was all she had to get the perfect part.

Chapter 3

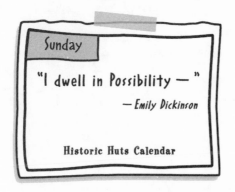

Sunday

"I dwell in Possibility — "
— *Emily Dickinson*

Historic Huts Calendar

I would prefer to dwell in Certainty. Then I would know what role I am going to get. Just to make sure I get one I want, I am rehearsing several of them. That is a lot of Possibility! It is also a lot of work!

11 days until the audition!

Abby's Acting Practice Journal
Laughed evilly.
Hid left hand in sleeve and walked with a rollicking gait.

Snarled.

Said "I won't grow up!" about a billion times.

Pretended to talk to fairies named Tinker-bell.

Practiced sword fighting.

Read stories to "Lost Boy" Alex.

Conclusion: I am very confused. Who am I? Am I mean and evil? A kid who doesn't want to grow up? Or a sweet older sister? (Ha! I wish I had one - or two - of those!)

News flash!

The Hayes family says it supports Abby Hayes's goals and aspirations. Paul Hayes tells his daughter she can do anything she wants. Olivia Hayes quotes her Working Woman's Wisdom Calendar about "reaching for the stars." Eva Hayes tells Abby to "go for the gold." Isabel says, "Anything worth doing is worth doing well." Alex

Hayes tells Abby that she will be the best ever.

However, when Abby Hayes starts to practice, the Hayes family becomes less understanding. They do not comprehend the demands of the stage. They do not encourage the young actress to reach perfection.

When Abby Hayes begins reading the script with a powerful, ringing interpretation of her three chosen roles, Isabel bangs on her bedroom door and demands that she tone down the noise. She says it's disturbing her study time.

Question: Is her study time more important than Abby's rehearsal time?

Another question: Is it possible to rehearse in a whisper? Whispering makes every line sound as if it's spoken by Tinkerbell.

Abby Hayes practiced dancing after dinner. Her own room was too cluttered with clothes on the floor, books, and piles of calendars to do more than a quick tiptoe across it, so she went into the living room.

She did pirouettes and pliés. She leaped across the room.

Instead of offering encouragement and praise, her SuperSister Eva told Abby to stop crashing into the furniture. She said it made her dizzy to watch. She said she was going to do calisthenics and the living room was reserved for <u>her</u>. When Abby protested this injustice, Eva said she had signed up for the space two days in advance.

Question: Since when does the Hayes family have a sign-up sheet for the living room?

Prevented from perfecting her ballet techniques, Abby decided to watch the movie <u>Peter Pan</u>. She had barely begun to watch for the second time when her mother, Olivia Hayes, told her to turn the television off.

"I'm studying the film!" Abby protested. "This is schoolwork!"

Olivia Hayes was not impressed. "You've watched too much television tonight, Abby."

"But, Mom," Abby eloquently argued.

"There's a historical drama on in fifteen minutes," Isabel interrupted. "I'm not missing it! It's about the Hundred Years' War."

"Wait a minute!" Eva said. "<u>I'm</u> planning to watch basketball."

"Too bad," Isabel said, turning the television to her channel.

Eva changed the channel again.

Question: Why isn't there a sign-up sheet for the television?

Abby did not stay to see what was going to happen. She did not want to be hit with a piece of shrapnel from the Hundred Years' War — or the Hundred Wars of Eva and Isabel. She left for her room.

After the play, the Hayes family will line up outside Abby's dressing room to apologize. She will graciously forgive them — after reminding them how they failed to recognize her acting genius.

P.S. Someone should issue frequent fighters coupons to my sisters. For every hundred fights, win

Frequent Fighter Coupon
for every 100 fights
win a free fight
or the argument of your choice!

a free fight or the argument of your choice.

Sign up today!!!

* * *

In the afternoon, I went to Jessica's house to rehearse.

Good thing.

Jessica has no annoying older sisters.

We made all the noise we wanted, and her mother didn't complain. (It helped that she was in the basement doing laundry.)

Natalie came over in the middle of the afternoon. She said her parents are threatening to make her join the basketball team. They think she spends too much time in her room doing experiments and reading Harry Potter books.

Natalie put on green leggings and stood on the couch, pretending to be Peter Pan. We thought she was! She inspired me to new heights as Captain

Hook. Or maybe new depths.

Then we switched roles. I was Peter Pan and she was Captain Hook. That was fun, too. Jessica narrated the story with a wheeze. It was hard for her to breathe because of an asthma attack the night before.

After we rehearsed, we had cookies and hot chocolate. Jessica makes great hot chocolate!

I need to do a lot more work on my singing, dancing, and acting to be ready to meet the Brianna challenge at the audition. With the help of my friends, I will succeed.

After dinner tonight, made second request for dance lessons. No luck. Will get dance video from library instead.

Chapter 4

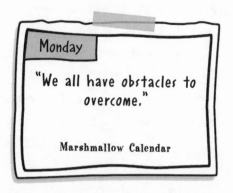

Monday

"We all have obstacles to overcome."

Marshmallow Calendar

Boy, do we ever! Why doesn't anyone ever tell us <u>how</u> to overcome the obstacles?? Huh? I want to know!! They just tell us that the obstacles are there. That's NOT a lot of help. Someone ought to have figured that out by now.

What I'd really like is a Solution-a-Day Calendar. Or an Answer to Every Problem Calendar. If they had a fifth-grade girls' edition, I'd buy a hundred copies!

Audition countdown: 10 days!

My problems:

To learn to sing, dance, and act in under two weeks!

To wow Ms. Bunder and Ms. Kantor with my reading.

To get a starring role in the play!

To dazzle everyone with my performance — especially Grandma Emma.

My solutions:

Took allowance and bought Ballet Calendar (identical to one I gave Brianna for her birthday), Sopranos of the South Calendar, and Peter Pan Calendar. Am studying them for clues that will help in my performance.

Watched dance video. Tried to imitate dancers' movements. Graceful arm gestures, toes pointed out, sudden leaps.

On third leap, banged leg on table. Got black-and-blue mark on shin.

Decided to sing instead. Put on tape of music for <u>Peter Pan</u>. Sang along.

Couldn't hit high notes. Squeaked and squawked.

Decided to practice breathing exercises that singers do, instead. Breathed deeply. Inhale, exhale. Inhale, exhale. Got dizzy. Fell on floor.

Decided to stop practicing.

Wrote letter to Grandma Emma instead.

Ms. Kantor, the fifth-grade-classroom teacher, clapped her hands. "All right! Everyone return to their desks!" she said.

The reading groups broke up. Abby gathered up her papers, returned a book to the shelf, and went back to her desk.

"Ms. Kantor! Ms. Kantor!" Brianna raised her hand.

"Yes, Brianna?" Ms. Kantor wore slacks and a sweater and comfortable sneakers. She had blond hair and a pointy nose. She had transferred from Swiss Hill Elementary; this was her first year at Lancaster.

Abby was glad that Ms. Kantor was new to their

school; it was good to have a teacher who didn't rave about her older sisters. To Ms. Kantor, Abby was just another student. She didn't have to live up to the megabrain of Isabel, or the megamuscles of Eva.

Brianna flipped her shiny dark hair over her shoulder. "Could we have an acting class? Not for me, of course." She smiled. "I've been taking classes since I was four. But some of the kids here don't have any idea how to read or rehearse. I want to make sure I act in a really professional production."

Ms. Kantor nodded her head. "That's a good idea, Brianna. We're going to work on geography projects next. Afterward, we'll have time to talk about the play. Maybe you can give everyone some acting tips."

"I'd love to, Ms. Kantor," Brianna smirked.

Abby pulled her journal onto her lap.

What are Brianna's acting tips? Always be the best? Make sure everyone knows it?

How can we all be the best when _she's_ the best? Maybe we have to be second best. Does that mean we try harder? Or that Brianna brags harder?

I agree with Brianna. An acting class would be great. But I don't want Brianna teaching it.

As Ms. Kantor passed out sheets of paper for the geography project, Zach hummed the pirate song from *Peter Pan*.

A mischievous look passed over Natalie's face. She slipped her hand inside her desk. A tiny bell sounded.

"We have Tinkerbell with us today," Ms. Kantor observed. "I'm glad to see so much enthusiasm for the play. Hold on to it for another hour."

Zach stuck out his tongue at Natalie. She made a face back at him.

Brianna scowled at both of them. She didn't like it when Zach paid any kind of attention to another girl.

"Now, for geography this week, we're each going to create an island," Ms. Kantor continued. "I want you to map out fields, forests, hills, cities, and roads. You should use the symbols we've been studying. I want you to think about the climate of the island, too, as well as the kinds of food people eat and the clothing they wear."

Abby stared at the blank piece of paper in front of her. Normally, she loved blank pieces of paper. They were meant to be filled with writing. Writing was what she loved to do best. But this was mapmaking! It was very precise. She liked to draw, but she didn't like rules about what she had to draw. She wished she could write about the island instead of mapping it.

"We'll start today with sketches and a rough draft. Next Wednesday, I expect a full-color map with lots of details," Ms. Kantor said.

Next Wednesday? That was one day before the tryouts! As if Abby didn't have enough to think about!

"When it rains, it pours," she said to herself. She had read that this morning in her Cute 'n Cuddly Cat Calendar. Ms. Kantor ought to hand out umbrellas!

Jessica was already bent over her paper, sketching her island with a sharp pencil. She looked happy. She had already given her island a name, and she probably knew its exact population, chief exports, and seasonal climate. This was just the kind of assignment that Jessica thrived on.

Abby quietly opened her journal again.

*No wonder they call it a rough draft!
Maybe it should even be called a tough
draft! Or a rough, tough draft.*

*I don't want to think about this island!
I'd rather think about Mermaid Island, in
Never-Never-Land. Could I do a map of
Mermaid Island for the assignment? I
don't think so. Mermaids, pirates, fairies,
and flying boys are not scientific.*

Anyway, what would they export? Fairy dust?

"Abby?" It was Ms. Kantor.

She quickly shut her journal and picked up her pencil.

"Get to work," Ms. Kantor said. "Unless you want to do the assignment at home, where I won't be able to help you if you have a question."

Ms. Kantor didn't know about Isabel. Abby's older sister was a walking dictionary/encyclopedia/book of knowledge. Then again, Ms. Kantor was right. Abby had to work on it now. At home, rehearsing was her first priority.

"I can't think of what kind of island to draw," she said.

"You?" Ms. Kantor laughed. "With your imagination? Come on, Abby! You can do it!"

Abby stared at the blank piece of paper some more. Jessica had already started to sketch in rivers and lakes. Natalie was humming as she drew a mountain range, which she had named Hogwarts, after Harry Potter's school. Zach and Tyler were working on islands called Gamer's Island and Computer Paradise. Brianna was smiling as she drew Brianna's Isle. Abby couldn't see Bethany's paper, but she bet *her* island was called "Yay, Brianna!"

What should she do? She thought of her sisters. No, she didn't want to think of her sisters. They would do something perfectly wonderful, especially Isabel. Her father? He would map it all out on the computer. Her brother, Alex, would have every relationship of water, land, and people worked out, even though he was only in second grade. He would probably design solar-heated houses and gravity-powered wells, too.

When Ms. Kantor clapped her hands again, Abby was still staring glumly at her desk.

Jessica shot her a sympathetic look. "Don't worry, you'll get it," she whispered.

"Does anyone have questions about the map?" Ms. Kantor asked.

"Plenty," Abby said under her breath.

"Abby?" Ms. Kantor asked.

Abby shook her head. What was there to say? That her brain cells had gone on strike? That her imagination was out to lunch? That she had just experienced sudden brain failure?

She promised herself to work on the map tonight. Maybe one of her sisters, or even her little brother, would help her. There were times when geniuses in the family came in handy.

Five minutes later, Brianna stood at the front of the class, smiling smugly. "Observe," she said.

She clasped her hands, looked out the window, and began to speak.

"I wonder if Peter Pan will visit the nursery tonight," she said. "Michael? John? Are you ready to hear the stories?" She gazed lovingly at two invisible brothers, then took a deep breath, faced the class, and began to whirl back and forth.

"I can fly!" she cried. "I will never grow up!"

She mimed a sword fight. "Take that, Captain Hook!"

Brianna stopped suddenly, took another breath, then fluttered delicately around the room.

The fifth-graders watched Brianna in complete silence. When she bowed to the class after having done Wendy, Peter Pan, Tinkerbell, and Mrs. Darling in the space of five minutes, everyone began to applaud.

"Bravo!" yelled Bethany. "Yay, Brianna!"

"Well! That was *excellent!*" Ms. Kantor said. "Can you give us some hints about how to approach our roles?"

Abby exchanged glances with Jessica and Natalie. "Who ever heard of Wendy in bump-toed boots and rhinestone pants?" she whispered. "Or Peter Pan in a camisole?"

"I didn't even think about what she was wearing," Jessica said. "She's *really* good."

"Yeah," Natalie agreed.

Abby sighed. "I know. It's true. How will any of us ever get parts in the play?"

"She can only play one role," Jessica reminded her.

"It'll probably be the one I want!" Abby slipped her journal into her backpack. She couldn't give up. After all, anything might happen. Brianna might come down with the measles. Or twist her ankle. Or get laryngitis. In ten days, Abby might become an acting genius. Who knew what surprises lay in store for them all?

Chapter 5

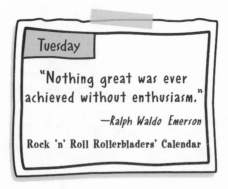

Tuesday

"Nothing great was ever achieved without enthusiasm."
—Ralph Waldo Emerson

Rock 'n' Roll Rollerbladers' Calendar

If that's true, then I should get whatever part I want! I have enough enthusiasm to fill all the oceans!

9 days to practice!

Pieces of acting advice Brianna gave the class: 3.

Number of times she said the words "I," "me," and "best" while giving advice: 27

Number of times she looked at Zach: 15

Number of times Zach looked back at her: 2

Roles she is going to try out for: Peter Pan and Wendy

How many others in the class admitted to wanting those roles: none

How many kids secretly want those roles: half the class — especially me!

Brianna's Best Acting Advice:

1. Observe others.

2. Use their mannerisms to bring characters to life.

3. <u>Become</u> the character. Think, eat, breathe, and laugh like the character. How would Peter Pan eat breakfast? What would Captain Hook say if he saw the SuperSisters fighting? How would Wendy do her homework?

(Note to self: Not good idea to do all characters at once. Might become split personality. Would end up in hospital ward. Would not be able to show up for audition.)

Maybe I should become Brianna! That is

the way to get her experience!

How to become Brianna:

1. Brag.

2. Brag.

3. Brag.

4. Flip hair.

5. Brag some more.

When Abby came down to breakfast, she was surprised to see her entire family sitting around the breakfast table.

"Mom?" Abby said. "Aren't you going to work?" Usually her mother had left or was leaving for the office just as Abby woke up.

Olivia Hayes checked her watch. She was wearing a pale-gray wool suit with a cream-colored silk blouse. Her hair was caught up in a sleek bun, and she wore a plain gold chain around her neck.

"Not this morning. I'm going to to talk to Eva and Isabel's class about what it's like to be a lawyer."

"Here you are, Abby," her father said. He poured her a glass of orange juice and pointed to a plate of French toast. "Help yourself. There's lots left."

"I invited her," Isabel announced. She wore a long

black velour spandex skirt with a jeans jacket worn over an electric-blue Lycra T-shirt. Her nails were painted blue to match.

"I made all the arrangements with the school," Eva added quickly. As usual, she looked as different from her twin as possible. She wore khaki pants and a zipped, hooded sweatshirt. "I made sure all the classes know about it. You'll have a big audience, Mom."

"Great." Olivia Hayes spread some jam on a piece of French toast. "The more the merrier."

"It was my idea in the first place," Isabel reminded her twin.

"Oh, yeah?" Eva retorted.

Abby's twin sisters were usually at the high school by the time Abby came down for breakfast. That was just fine with Abby. It made the start of the day much more peaceful and relaxed.

Their mother held up her hand. "Remember your promise," she said to the twins.

"What promise?" Alex asked sleepily. He was dressed neither for fashion nor comfort. In fact, he was barely dressed at all. His pajama top was half unbuttoned. He had on jeans, and one worn slipper on his left foot. Next to his plate was an old modem that he had begun to take apart.

"We're not going to fight today," Isabel and Eva chorused in unison. "That's what we promised as a thank-you to Mom for visiting the school."

"Wow," Alex said.

"It's a unilateral peace treaty," Isabel said as she poured herself a cup of coffee.

"It's plain old good sportsmanship," Eva insisted. "You shouldn't drink that stuff," she said to her twin. "It's not good for you."

Isabel glared at her. Instead of firing off one of her usual missiles, however, she grabbed the plate of French toast and helped herself to another piece.

Paul and Olivia Hayes smiled at each other. "Such a pleasant breakfast," Olivia said. "Thanks for making the French toast, honey."

Abby shook her head. She couldn't believe it. Could Isabel and Eva actually go five seconds without a fight? They needed to fight the way they needed to breathe. She had never before seen them exercise such self-control.

"Would you please pass the orange juice, Isabel?" Eva asked sweetly.

"Of course, Eva. Have another piece of French toast," her twin replied even more sweetly.

"Thank you, Isabel."

"You're welcome, Eva."

If Eva and Isabel could stop fighting for even ten minutes, *anything* was possible. Pigs could fly, the moon could be made of blue cheese, and Abby could be Wendy, Peter Pan, and Captain Hook all at once.

"Thanks, Eva and Isabel!" Abby said. "You're the greatest!"

"Sure," Eva said. She was so used to getting compliments, she never even questioned why she got them.

"Thanks for what?" Isabel demanded. She got as many compliments as Eva, but she always had to know why.

"You've given me hope for the future." Abby poured a generous helping of maple syrup over her French toast.

"Huh?" Isabel said.

Abby began to sing. "I won't grow up!"

"You won't grow up?" her mother teased. "Does that mean you don't want pierced ears anymore?"

"No!" Abby yelled. "I mean, yes! I *want* pierced ears. It's just a song from *Peter Pan*, Mom."

Her mother grinned at her, enjoying the joke.

Everyone was in a good mood this morning. It was probably because of the Twin Truce. Maybe now was the right time to ask for lessons. She had already asked two times. Maybe three would be a charm.

"Mom? Dad?" Abby said. "Do you think I could have singing lessons? Brianna's been taking them since she was three. She also takes dancing lessons, acting lessons, French lessons, *and* has pierced ears."

"A few holes in the head, huh?" Isabel commented. "Probably needs a place for the hot air to exit."

For once, Isabel had said something that Abby could agree with.

Her father frowned. "You can't catch up to Brianna in only a few short weeks."

"Lessons? For a school play?" her mother said.

"But I have to do something if I want to get a good part!" Abby cried.

Her parents exchanged glances.

"Please, Mom and Dad? Can I have *any* kind of lessons?"

"We'll have to discuss it," her mother said. "We can't give you an answer right now."

Abby's mother knew a thousand ways to delay committing herself to a decision. It was part of her legal training.

"Mom!" Abby cried.

"Wait a minute." Isabel blew on her nails and gave them a quick shine with her napkin. "I studied voice with an opera singer in sixth and seventh grades. Only five kids in my class were selected. Why don't I give Abby some singing lessons?"

Abby stared at her sister in horror. "Can't I take lessons with a professional?" she begged.

"Don't worry; I'm good," Isabel said confidently.

"I'm sure you are, honey," their mother agreed.

"We'll work on your breathing, your vowels, and a few scales," Isabel promised. "We'll start to-night."

Everyone beamed at Isabel. Especially Eva. "You're a sport, Sis," she said.

Isabel smiled between clenched teeth. Everyone knew she hated being called a sport.

"There's the solution to all your problems, Abby," her father said. "It takes time to find a good teacher, you know. Get started with your sister, and then, if you want to continue, we'll find someone to give you lessons."

The solution to all her problems? No! It was the beginning of all Abby's problems! Even if she was stuck on a desert island and her older sister was the only human around for thousands of miles, Abby *still* wouldn't want know-it-all SuperSib Genius Isabel to coach her in anything.

Chapter 6

Thursday

"Genius is patience."
— Proverb

Paper Clip Calendar

Oh, yeah? Without <u>im</u>patience, nothing would ever get done. The auditions are only one week away, and I am impatient to master my roles. That is why I have done the following things.

7 days until A day!

Practiced <u>becoming</u> different characters. This is fun.

At breakfast yesterday, I became a piece of buttered toast. Felt dryness at my edges where no one buttered me. Enjoyed the feeling of melting butter over my middle. Cried when Eva ate me.

Was mourning the death of toast, when I became cold cereal. I was one of many marshmallow letters of the alphabet being poured into Alex's bowl. My friends and I tumbled together in the bowl, until suddenly I was floating in a sea of milk. Then a silver scoop pulled us out of the water and into the air, toward the wide-open mouth of a giant. Cried again when Alex ate me.

(My family now thinks I am crazy.)

Observed others. Tried to create new and exciting interpretation of roles.

Alex chews with mouth open. Will this be useful to any of my characters? Not unless I play Michael or John.

Eva flexes her muscles every five minutes. Very annoying habit. Who would do it?

Captain Hook? Play him as superjock who dislikes superbrain, Peter Pan?

Isabel constantly a) looks at her nails (to reassure herself they are still there and have not flown to someone else's hands?) b) blows on her nails (for good luck?) and c) buffs her nails (so she can use them as mirrors?).

Is Wendy also obsessed by fingernails? Does she check her nail polish as she reads stories to the Lost Boys?

Jessica fiddles with her asthma inhaler a lot. Does Peter Pan have asthma? Maybe that's why he doesn't want to grow up — he's afraid his asthma will get worse.

Asked Jessica what she thought of this. She said it wasn't realistic. Usually kids outgrow their asthma. If Peter Pan had asthma, he'd <u>want</u> to grow up!

Decided to use Natalie as model for Peter Pan. He is flying away from parents who make him join sports teams even though he hates sports. Must go to Never-Never-Land, where he can perform chemistry experiments and read Harry Potter books all day.

Watched video again. Noticed that Peter Pan brags a lot. Is it because he can fly? Or because he has a lot of Lost Boys obeying his slightest command? Reminds me of Brianna. (Except <u>her</u> Peter Pan would lead the Best Boys!)

Singing. This is where that "genius is patience" stuff comes in.
Especially when Isabel gives me a lesson.
She made me read the songs over and over.
"I <u>know</u> how to read," I told her. "I want to learn to sing."
"Speaking out loud is the first step to singing," she pronounced.
"I know how to speak," I said.
Isabel didn't seem to care.
After reading the songs out loud about a hundred times, she finally let me sing.

I started with the flying song. "Think about how it feels to fly when you sing it," Isabel said.

Began to flutter arms. Felt myself lift into air. My curly red hair fluttering in the wind. Just as I was really beginning to soar, I tripped on ball. (Why do balls lie around on floors, anyway? Sometimes it seems like they're waiting for you on purpose.)

Isabel said that I wasn't actually <u>supposed</u> to fly; I was just supposed to imagine it.

"Put the flying in your voice, not your feet," she said.

"What if my voice flies away?" I asked.

Older sister got annoyed. "I'm doing this as a favor to you, Abby, and you're not cooperating."

Must be very patient with Isabel when she gives me voice lessons.

(She thinks <u>she</u> is the one being patient with me!)

"I *love* her earrings," Abby said to Jessica as Ms. Bunder walked into the classroom. "Aren't they cute?"

"Me, too," Jessica agreed. She doodled a picture of an alien with long dangling earrings in the margin of her notebook.

It was Thursday morning, time for the weekly creative-writing class. Not only was Ms. Bunder Abby's all-time favorite teacher of her all-time favorite subject, she also wore great clothes and jewelry.

Today she wore a ribbed scoop-neck top and a long skirt with a daisy pattern on it. Around her neck was a silver daisy necklace. Her earrings matched the necklace.

Natalie nudged Abby and Jessica. "Look," she said, pointing to Brianna.

Brianna was taking notes on Ms. Bunder's outfit.

"I bet she has notebooks full of them," Abby whispered. "Maybe she opened up the June notebook by mistake this week; that's why she keeps wearing sleeveless dresses in the cold."

Ms. Bunder clapped her hands for attention.

"I have your last assignment here," she said, pointing to a stack of papers. "You all did a great job."

That was another thing Abby loved about Ms. Bunder: She was so enthusiastic! She made everyone feel excited about writing and what they could do with it. Especially Abby!

When she handed out writing journals, she had given Abby her favorite color, purple. Sometimes she teased Abby and called her "Purple Hayes" because she wrote with a purple pen in a purple notebook.

Brianna raised her hand. "Ms. Bunder, instead of doing a writing assignment, can we work on our roles for *Peter Pan* today?"

A mixed chorus of yeses and nos rose from the class.

"Yes!" cried Bethany, Natalie, Zach, and Tyler.

"No!" cried Jessica, Rachel, Jon, and Collin.

Abby didn't know what to say. On the one hand, she needed all the help she could get if she wanted to land a starring role next week.

On the other, she did *not* want to miss a minute of creative writing. It was an oasis in the middle of a desert of math homework, spelling tests, and geography assignments.

"Sorry, Brianna," Ms. Bunder picked up last week's assignments and began to return them to the students. "This hour is for writing."

Abby breathed a sigh of relief.

"We're going to write letters today," Ms. Bunder continued. "If you want to write a letter about the play, go ahead."

"Ugh! My mother makes me write thank-you letters all the time," Tyler groaned. "I don't want to write any more."

"Let's have fun," Ms. Bunder said. "Be playful. We can write to a character in a book, to a favorite author, to a friend, or to someone we admire. Our letters can be funny, imaginary, or true."

"How about a letter to ourselves?" Brianna asked.

"Why not?" Ms. Bunder said.

"A letter to a computer-game character?" Zach suggested.

Ms. Bunder nodded. "As long as it's a letter. Remember: The purpose of a letter is to communicate. Think about what you want to say and to whom you want to say it."

That was another thing Abby loved about Ms. Bunder. She was willing to consider any idea, no matter how different. She appreciated imagination.

The fifth-graders picked up their pens and began to write. Everyone in the class had something to communicate.

Dear Isabel,
Thanks for the singing lessons. They are very good. I might even like them if someone else was teaching them. . . .
Dear Isabel,
This is to inform you that your services as a singing teacher will no longer be required. . . .
Dear Isabel,
You're fired!

She crumpled the sheet and got out a new one.

"Abby? You haven't started?" Ms. Bunder handed her a paper with a rainbow star on the top. It was last week's assignment, a story that Abby had written in the form of a poem.

"False start, Ms. Bunder," Abby explained.

Ms. Bunder nodded her head as if she understood.

Abby picked up her pen again. Forget about Isabel! She'd write to her favorite grandmother! Her grandmother was the main reason she wanted to star in the play. She'd be so proud and happy to see Abby on stage!

Dear Grandma Emma,
Do hard work and perseverance lead to success? If so, I should be a star very soon.

The words came more and more quickly. There was so much to tell her grandmother! She wondered if Grandma Emma would read the letter to her dog, Zipper.

Chapter 7

I wish I was. Then Isabel would have to row over to see me. Maybe she would get shipwrecked on another island on the way over. Then she would give singing lessons to the fish. (Ha-ha.)

My dad said that there is an Isle of Man. Why isn't there also an Isle of Animals? Or an Isle of Plants? What about an Isle of Kids?

Speaking of islands, I better get started

on mine. Was going to ask Isabel for help, but every time she sees me, she gives me singing advice.

5 more days . . . .

Help! I am being pursued by a crazed older sister who makes me sing scales at the breakfast table in front of the entire family. After school, she barges into my room and tells me to breathe from my stomach.

Have told her I don't want any more lessons. She said, "Fine," but she keeps giving advice.

Have also noticed her taking notes. Is Isabel writing research paper with me as subject? Am suspicious. Am also dizzy from all the breathing exercises.

Finally got island idea. Will create an island for Grandma Emma. That way, will finish the geography assignment _and_ give it to grandmother as a present when she arrives.

My dad, when I told him, said that I had killed two birds with one stone.

"I'd never kill one bird with a stone!" I protested.

He said it was just an expression. It means accomplishing two goals with one action.

"How about two for the price of one?" he said.

"I'm not buying anything," I pointed out.

"Well, I like your idea of doing your assignment and creating a present at the same time. It shows that you're thinking. You have a sharp mind, Abby."

"Thanks, Dad."

Nice compliment from Dad. May forgive him for forcing me to take singing lessons from Isabel.

Note to self: Why are minds sharpened or dulled? Why are they compared to knives and not forks? Can a mind be piercing? Or scoop like a spoon? My mind is wandering like a cursor on a computer screen. Must click back on main subject.

What is main subject?

Abby's Acting Journal

Ha! Ha! Ha!

Peals of insane laughter are heard offstage as Captain Hook waves his sword
and vows vengeance on Peter Pan, the boy
who spends all his spare time in the library
and aces every test.

The soothing voice of Wendy, older sister
of Michael and John, is telling stories
about Peter Pan. She is sitting in a big,
comfortable chair and looking out the window at the stars. Every now and then, she
stares at her fingernails and blows on them
to dry the latest coat of polish.

"Do you think I can fly?" Peter Pan asks
Wendy. He needs to have his confidence
built up.

"If you believe it, you can fly," Wendy
says. She climbs onto a table, opens her
arms, and floats across the room. Her glittery nails sparkle in the moonlight.

Peter Pan stares at her in awe. He asks
her to come home with him to Mermaid Island, which he created for a geography assignment. (He got the highest grade awarded

in his school. No one had ever before created an actual island!) He tells Wendy he
needs her to round up the Lost Boys, who
have gotten, well, lost.

Wait a minute. Wait a minute! <u>WAIT</u> a
minute!
I am not preparing my roles; I am
rewriting the play!!!
Must concentrate.
Must focus.
Must practice parts as they <u>are</u>; not as
they could be!
I can do it, I can, I can! If I believe
it, I can fly <u>and</u> act.

Decided to call friends and rehearse with
them to keep me on track.
Jessica was about to go shopping with
her mother for winter boots and couldn't
rehearse.
Natalie was free. She came over with
props: a sword, a pirate hat, and a cape.
(They were from her brother's room; he is at

boarding school, so he won't find out. Some people are lucky. They don't live with older siblings who make their lives miserable.)

Told Natalie about the changes I wanted to make to play. "I think Peter Pan is a brain who ran away from home," I said. "And Wendy is a know-it-all who checks her nail polish every fifteen minutes."

Natalie laughed. She thought it was funny but agreed we should rehearse the play as it was. Otherwise we might not get the parts we want.

Rehearsed play in my living room. (No SuperSibs in sight. They were at games, libraries, and friends' houses.)

Dad came in when we were rehearsing the sword-fight scene and watched for a while. He told me I am improving.

Hooray!

Then he asked Natalie what part she was trying out for.

"John or Michael," Natalie said. She pushed her short hair back from her face.

"Don't I look like a boy?"

Dad smiled and said, "You look like Peter Pan to me, Natalie."

"Really?" She thought about it for a moment, then shook her head. "I don't think so."

"You should try out for the role," my father advised her. "You're a natural actor."

Natalie looked at him like she couldn't believe it.

I couldn't believe it, either. My father was supposed to say those words to <u>me</u>!

"What's stopping you?" my father said to her. "Go for it! You have the talent!"

"What about me?" I demanded. "I want to be Peter Pan, too."

"I thought you wanted to be Wendy," my father said.

"That wimp?" I lied. "Never!"

"You'll find a role you like," he said to me. "You should sign up for an acting class," he told Natalie.

"What???" I felt breathless, as if someone had knocked the air from my lungs.

Was this how Jessica felt when she had an asthma attack? My father was telling Natalie to join an acting class, when he told _me_ I couldn't have one!

Natalie didn't notice that I was upset. She looked happy. "I act things out in my room," she told my father. "I pretend I'm different characters from the Harry Potter books."

"I'll be rooting for you, Natalie," my father said.

"What about me?" I said.

He gave me a hug. "Of course I'm rooting for you, Abby. That goes without saying."

"Brianna's going to be Peter Pan," I warned him. "She has years of acting experience. She'll get whatever she wants. Natalie doesn't have much of a chance."

"Don't be so sure about that," my father said. "Surprises happen."

Do they ever! Like fathers becoming traitors and encouraging friends instead of self!

Why My Father Encouraged Natalie and Not Me:
1. I'm so good I don't need any praise.
   (I don't believe this.)
2. She's not very good, and he was trying to boost her spirits.
   (I don't believe this, either.)
3. He's trying to break it to me gently:
   I'm a terrible actress and should give
   up all hope of appearing onstage.
   (This might be true, though I hope it
   isn't.)
4. He doesn't love me anymore and secretly wants another daughter who is
   gifted like the twins.
   (No comment.)
5. He thinks Natalie has lots of talent.
   And I don't.
   (Boo hoo.)
Pick the correct answer and win a trip to
Never-Never-Land with all expenses paid!

* * *

It isn't Natalie's fault. She is really a nice person. She's not conceited at all—and still isn't, even after my father gave her so many compliments. I shouldn't be mad at her. I won't be mad at her. I won't!! I will be <u>really</u> mad at my father!

When will Jessica be back from her shopping trip? She has probably bought fifteen pairs of boots by now. I need to talk to her!!

No one answers at her house, so I have to talk to my journal instead.

Note to journal: Do not be offended that I sometimes want to talk to my best friend instead of you. Am sure you will be understanding.

Chapter 8

Monday

"Time is man's angel."
—Friedrich von Schiller

Snowy Roads Calendar

Is time my angel or my tormentor? Do I have enough time to make myself good enough to win a lead role?

Now that I've written to Grandma Emma and told her that I'm going to get a big role, I can't disappoint her. Or me.

Audition countdown: 3 days! That's all! I have decided to ignore my father. What does he know about acting, anyway? When I am a star, he'll be sorry!

Must become star of stage, if not screen. Must, must, must! Will, will, will!

"Practice makes perfect." That is what my mother always says. But <u>what</u> does it make perfect? My acting? Or something else, like fake crying?

<u>Abby's Acting Practice</u>

Hid in closet to avoid singing advice from Isabel. (She keeps telling me to sing numbers! What next? The alphabet?)

Fenced with Eva's lacrosse stick in front of mirror. Got it back in her room before she noticed that I had borrowed it.

Conducted secret acting exercises. At dinner, pretended that I had just arrived from Never-Never-Land. Laughed because of a joke Peter Pan had told me. Flicked fairy dust from my sleeves.

Family's reaction:

Eva: Do you have dandruff?

Mother: I don't know why you're laughing, Abby; you forgot to unload the dishwasher this afternoon. Now you'll have twice as much work to do after supper.

Alex: Will you play chess with me tonight?

Isabel: She can't. She has to practice her vowels.

Abby: I learned them in kindergarten.

Isabel ignored this vital piece of information.

Father: Is Natalie going to audition for the role of Peter Pan? Try to encourage her, Abby.

Excused myself from table. Went to room and read biography of famous actor who overcame discouragement and many obstacles to arrive at stardom.

"You're sure you don't want to come with us?" Jessica asked one more time.

"I'm staying in," Abby said firmly. She shuffled some papers on her desk. "I have to finish this."

"Okay," Jessica said. "I'm sorry." She reached in her pocket and pulled out a candy bar. "Here. Have a piece of this chocolate."

Abby broke off a piece of chocolate and put it in her mouth. She waved to Jessica, who put on her coat and scarf and went out of the classroom. Then she pulled out her colored pencils and paper.

It was recess, and instead of going out with her friends, Abby had decided to stay in and work on Grandma Emma's Island. She hadn't done a thing over the weekend, and it was due on Wednesday.

Ms. Kantor sat at her desk, eating a sandwich and reading a book. Abby wondered what book it was. What did teachers read in their spare time? Not stories about school, she bet. Ms. Kantor probably liked to read about people who scaled mountains or crossed seas.

The classroom was silent. Abby picked up a green pencil and drew the outlines of a large island that almost filled the page. Grandma Emma liked to canoe and row. She liked to hike, too. Abby drew a lake, a mountain range, and a city where her grandmother would live. The city had plenty of parks for Zipper to run in.

She drew a white sandy beach along the shore, where her grandmother would swim. She drew roads from the city to the mountain ranges and lakes and seashore.

Was this a warm, tropical island or a cold, arctic one? Did the people live by growing bananas and pineapples or by exporting wool? One thing was for sure: If you lived on an island, you ate lots of fish. Abby drew fish in the sea surrounding the island.

She was almost finished. Why had it taken her so long, and why had she thought the assignment was so hard? It had been fun to do. All she had needed was a good idea.

Reaching into her backpack, Abby pulled out a shiny envelope decorated with pictures of couches. It was Grandma Emma's latest letter. She had just gotten it that morning.

Dear Abby,

So you're going to be a star! I always knew it. Can't wait to see you in the play! Today Zipper and I went for a walk along the waterfront. Then we stopped in a café for blueberry muffins and hot chocolate. Did you know that your cousin Cleo is also starring in a play? She is the Tin Man in The Wizard of Oz. *She wanted to borrow Zipper for the part of Toto, but I didn't think that Zipper would behave himself onstage. He would probably bark at the Cowardly Lion or jump on the Scarecrow.*

Only six more weeks! I have the date circled in purple, just like you do.

Lots of love from your Grandma Emma.

Abby smiled as she read the letter again and imagined Zipper onstage. He was a small, excitable dog who barked shrilly when he saw a stranger. No one in her right mind would let him near a stage. She wondered why cousin Cleo had wanted him in her play. She wondered if cousin Cleo was a talented actress. Had her parents let her take singing and dancing lessons before she auditioned for her part?

Her cousin Cleo was also in fifth grade. She lived near Grandma Emma and got to see her all the time. Abby wished that *she* lived near Grandma Emma. Then she would visit her every day and play with Zipper, too. She might even get to take him on walks and feed him.

"All done, Abby?" Ms. Kantor put down her book, threw out the remains of her sandwich, and wrote the week's spelling words on the board.

"Yes, I finished!" Abby colored in the last flower

in the border of tropical flowers she had drawn around the island. Then she wrote "Grandma Emma's Island" in rainbow colors at the bottom.

Checking over the assignment one last time to see if she had forgotten anything, Abby carried it over to Ms. Kantor.

"Nice work," her teacher said.

"I'm going to frame it and give it to my grandmother as a present when she comes to visit," Abby told her. "Her very own island!"

"I'm sure she'll love it."

The bell rang. The fifth-graders trooped back into the classroom. Their cheeks were red from the cold. Laughing and jostling, they pulled off their mittens and coats.

Abby made a thumbs-up sign to Jessica. "It's done."

"Yes!" Jessica said. Behind her, Natalie clapped.

"Did I miss anything?" Abby asked them.

"Brianna gave us an acting workshop," Bethany answered. She was wearing a white coat with a faux fur collar. There were snowflakes in her hair.

Tyler and Zach were right behind her. Tyler tiptoed up to Zach, who pretended to menace him. "We're Hook and Smee, pirates to be!" they chanted.

Brianna made her entrance into the classroom. She had a long scarf flung around her shoulders like a boa. "You missed my master class," she said to Abby.

"I had work to do," Abby said.

"What part are you going to audition for — Mrs. Darling? Nana?" Brianna asked Abby. "I'll give you pointers."

"I'm going to audition for Wendy," Abby announced. "And I don't want any pointers."

"Good luck," Brianna cooed. "It's *my* part — unless I decide I'm Peter Pan."

Abby exchanged glances with Jessica and Natalie. Brianna couldn't have the whole play to herself — or could she?

"Our teachers will decide," Abby reminded everyone. She hoped Ms. Kantor and especially Ms. Bunder wouldn't be too impressed by Brianna. She hoped that she and Natalie both got good parts.

Mrs. Kantor cleared her throat. "Sit down, everyone. We have a new spelling unit to go over."

As the fifth-graders filed back to their seats, Jessica dropped a note on Abby's desk. She opened it up. "Meet me and Natalie after school," it said. "We'll practice by ourselves."

Abby picked up her journal.

Brianna Brags Again! Wonder if she charged for her Master Class. Maybe she made Zach and Tyler give her cheat codes for computer games. Or did she collect everyone's ice-cream money?

Have decided not to try out for Captain Hook or Peter Pan. Will concentrate on Wendy. She is storyteller like me. Anyway, one role is more than enough to worry about. Especially if Brianna wants it!

Chapter 9

> **Wednesday**
>
> "Tomorrow,
> tomorrow . . ."
> —*Annie*
>
> **Days of Our Lives Calendar**

My mother sings this song — and those are the only words she knows. When I tell her I'm sick of hearing it, she sings a song called "Yesterday." What if she put the two together — would she get a song called "Today"?

Today I am nervous about tomorrow. Tomorrow are the auditions. They are happening in the afternoon. We are skipping math and geography (hooray!).

Today is my last chance to practice before tomorrow.

*　*　*

1 day left!

Number of times Jessica, Natalie, and I have rehearsed the play together: 12 (a low estimate)

Number of times I have sung EACH of the songs: 31 (no thanks to Isabel)

Number of times I have watched the video: 11

Number of dance routines I have practiced every day: 4

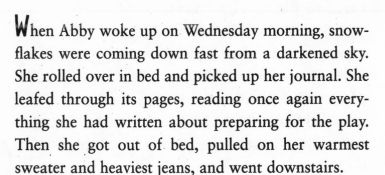

Do all these numbers add up to a starring role? Or do they add up to disappointment?

When Abby woke up on Wednesday morning, snowflakes were coming down fast from a darkened sky. She rolled over in bed and picked up her journal. She leafed through its pages, reading once again everything she had written about preparing for the play. Then she got out of bed, pulled on her warmest sweater and heaviest jeans, and went downstairs.

In the kitchen, Isabel, still in her bathrobe, was pouring cereal into a bowl.

"Are you sick?" Abby asked. At this time of morning, Isabel was usually not only dressed, but in the library studying.

"Go back to bed," Isabel said. "A big storm is coming. School's canceled."

A snow day! Abby loved them. It was so cozy to stay home and watch the snow fall. She liked to drink hot chocolate and read a book and then, later on, go outside and help her father shovel snow. Today, however, she wasn't as thrilled as usual.

"Is it supposed to snow tomorrow, too?" She hoped not. What would happen to the audition if school was canceled? Ms. Bunder came only on Thursdays. They couldn't wait another week! If the auditions and the play had to be rescheduled, Grandma Emma might miss it!

"I don't know." Isabel took her bowl to the table. "You never can tell what these storms will do."

"It better stop snowing by tomorrow! Or else!" Abby pulled the oatmeal down from the shelf. The trees and bushes in the backyard were thickly coated with snow. Outside, there was no rush of morning traffic.

"Where's Alex?" she asked.

"Went back to bed." Isabel pulled out the world news section from the newspaper and began to scan it. She had painted her nails a pale shade of yellow the night before. "Eva's getting ready to cross-country ski with her friends. I'm going to study for the history debate."

Abby stirred the oatmeal in the pot and sleepily wondered what actors ate for breakfast. Did they have special diets like athletes? At least she didn't have to drink revolting power health shakes to become a star of the stage.

She glanced again at the snowy yard and hoped again that the storm would be over before tomorrow.

"I'll never trust the weather reports again," their father said, coming into the kitchen. "They said an inch of snow last night, and now we have a blizzard on our hands."

"Are you going skiing today, Dad?" Isabel asked.

"No, work as usual," her father said. "When you have a home office, you don't have any excuses. I have a new program that's giving me lots of problems. I'm going to try to get it up and running."

Abby sat down with her bowl of oatmeal.

"What about you, Abby?" he asked. "Going to spend the day with Jessica or Natalie?"

"Maybe." She hadn't completely forgiven her father. Natalie was a good actor, it was true; she just wanted him to be equally enthusiastic about her acting. "I need to work on my role."

"You've practiced and rehearsed very hard for two weeks," her father said to Abby. "You've done a great job. Today you should relax, forget about the play, and have fun."

"Do you mean that, Dad?" Abby cried.

"Of course I mean it! Take the day off, and tomorrow you'll have a terrific audition. You'll get whatever part you want."

Isabel dusted an invisible speck from her nails. "If I were you, I'd be using every moment to prepare."

"You're wrong, Isabel," their father said. "It's always good to take a break. Then you come back refreshed."

"Do you really think I've done a great job, Dad?" Abby asked again.

Her father nodded.

She jumped up and hugged him.

"I can't wait to see the play," he said. "There's a lot of talent in Ms. Kantor's class!"

Outside, the snow fell thickly. Abby finished her oatmeal. The day stretched before her, with nothing to do but enjoy herself. She would call Jessica and Natalie and invite them over. Maybe Natalie's mother would let her take a bus by herself, or maybe she'd drive her over. She hoped her friends would be in the mood for a good old-fashioned snowball fight.

Chapter 10

Thursday

"The reward of a thing well done is to have done it."

— Ralph Waldo Emerson

Spuds Calendar

Rehearsing, practicing, and acting are <u>not</u> enough of a reward in themselves! I want more! I want to be Wendy. That will be my reward. I hope to have it by this afternoon.

Today is A day!

My father told me to "break a leg!" (Which one?)

Isabel reminded me to breathe. (Fat chance that I'll forget!)

Alex gave me his teddy
bear key chain for good luck.
My mother kissed me and
told me she knew I would do
well. (Mothers <u>always</u> say that.
Why? And <u>how</u> do they know?)
Eva was already at swim team practice,
so she couldn't add anything to the Hayes
family's good wishes.

I think I can, I think I can, I think I
can. Must remember I am Wendy, not the
Little Engine Who Could.

There is snow everywhere outside. We
have mountains of snow in the front yard.
But the sidewalks have narrow, shoveled
paths. The sky is clear and the roads are
plowed. School is NOT canceled. Hooray!
I can't wait to go to school today.

The Lancaster Elementary gym doubled as the
school auditorium. There was a stage at one end and
mats piled up at another. On Thursday afternoon, it

was filled with Ms. Kantor's fifth-graders, waiting to try out for the play.

Mr. Stevens, the gym teacher, stopped to watch the activity. "Can I have a part?" he asked jokingly.

"You can be Mr. Darling," Jessica said.

"He's the one who doesn't believe in Peter Pan," Mr. Stevens said. "I'd rather be a Lost Boy. They have all the fun."

"You're way too big," Abby pointed out. "You'd make the other Lost Boys look like dwarfs."

Mr. Stevens laughed. "I'll be part of the audience, then, and cheer the cast on."

Zach and Tyler pulled open the curtains.

There were stacks of chairs piled high at the back of the stage. Ms. Bunder and Ms. Kantor took two chairs and set them down near the front. Then Ms. Kantor clapped her hands for attention.

"Sit down, class!" she called. "Quiet, please!"

The fifth-graders sat cross-legged on the gym floor.

"Is everyone ready for the audition?" she asked. "Has everyone practiced their parts?"

"YES!" her fifth-graders roared in answer.

"Okay, let me tell you how this is going to work. We'll call you up one by one and ask you to read from your chosen part."

Abby, Jessica, and Natalie exchanged glances.

"While your classmates are onstage, give them your full attention," Ms. Kantor continued. "Clap after each person is done."

". . . and if you believe in fairies," Abby whispered to her friends.

"Tomorrow morning I'll announce the results."

A groan rose from the group.

"I know it's a long time to wait," Ms. Bunder said sympathetically. "Everyone will have a part."

Ms. Kantor added, "Not everyone is going to get the part they want, but we hope you'll be happy with the part you get."

"What if I don't get the part of Wendy?" Abby said in a panic to Jessica. "What if I have to be a Lost Boy or a pirate?"

"Don't worry," Jessica said. "You'll do great."

Abby closed her eyes, crossed her fingers, and whispered words of encouragement to herself. "You can do it," she murmured. "You can, you can, you can."

The audition began. One by one, the fifth-graders climbed onstage and read their lines.

Rachel and Jon read together for the parts of Mr.

and Mrs. Darling. Jon was a tall, husky boy with curly dark hair. He had a loud voice that boomed out over the gym.

As Mrs. Darling, Rachel, who was one of Brianna's friends, was brisk and matter-of-fact.

Ms. Bunder called Zach up.

He swaggered onstage and waved his left arm. A long hook protruded from his sleeve.

"I'm Captain Hook, and I'm going to get Peter Pan if it's the last thing I do," he snarled.

"Ooooh!" the audience gasped.

"He's pretty good, isn't he?" Natalie whispered to Abby and Jessica.

"Yeah," Abby agreed.

"I never knew Zach was so . . . dramatic," Brianna sighed. "Don't you agree, Bethany?"

Bethany nodded. "Tyler will be great as Smee, too," she said loudly. She glanced at him to see his reaction, but he wasn't listening.

"I can't wait to be onstage opposite Zach," Brianna said. "We'll have electrifying chemistry."

"The kind that explodes," Natalie muttered. "I know a thing or two about chemistry."

The reading was over. Zach walked off the stage, menacing the audience one last time with his hook.

The fifth-graders burst into loud applause.

"We'd like Brianna to come up next," Ms. Bunder said. "Are you ready, Brianna?"

"Of course I am," she announced. She marched onstage. Under her sweater and skirt she wore green leggings and a green top. In a moment, she had transformed herself.

"I thought you were trying out for the part of Wendy," Ms. Kantor said.

"I changed my mind." Brianna plopped a hat on her head, took a breath and, without a script, began to speak Peter Pan's lines.

"This is great for me," Abby whispered to Jessica, "but it's terrible for Natalie. She doesn't have a chance. Brianna is really, really good." She glanced at Natalie, who was watching Brianna intently. "I hope she's not too disappointed."

Brianna leaped across the stage like the ballet dancer that she was. She beamed at the audience. She sang in a high, pure voice, then beamed at everyone some more. Finally, she concluded her lines and bowed gracefully to Ms. Kantor and Ms. Bunder.

"Yay, Brianna!" Bethany yelled, clapping wildly.

With a gracious nod to her admirers, Brianna waltzed off the stage.

"I wouldn't like to play opposite Brianna," Jessica whispered. "She'd steal every scene."

"And say that it was someone else's fault," Abby concluded. If she got the part of Wendy, she might have to be onstage with Brianna. That would be the price of stardom.

"Abby!" Ms. Bunder was gesturing to her. "It's your turn!"

Her heart began to pound. Her head felt dizzy. This was the moment she had waited for. She rubbed Alex's teddy bear for good luck and got up.

"What part would you like to read?" Ms. Kantor asked as she climbed onto the stage.

"Wendy," Abby said. No one had auditioned for the part yet, thank goodness. If Abby had a chance to star in the play, this was it. She took three deep breaths, scanned the page that her teachers handed her, and began to read.

At first, her voice was wobbly, but then, suddenly, the words began to flow. She could almost see John and Michael opposite her, and even Peter Pan. She was aware of her classmates sitting on the floor a few feet away and Ms. Bunder and Ms. Kantor listening thoughtfully. As she read, she lopped off sentences and added new ones. It seemed completely natural to change the words from time to time. Wendy wouldn't say something this dumb, would she?

Then she was done. Ms. Kantor made a few notes on a piece of paper. Abby's arms and legs felt shaky. Above the applause, she heard Jessica and Natalie cheering.

"Very good, Abby." Ms. Bunder smiled at her.

She handed back the script, and weak with relief that it was finally over, she went back to her place.

"Great!" Jessica congratulated her.

"You were really good," Natalie agreed. "The best you've ever been."

"Really?" Her head was spinning. She was barely aware of Bethany, who was now onstage and flitting back and forth with a pair of pink fairy wings on her back. *"Really?"*

"Yes!" her friends said.

She sighed. Did other actors experience this when they got offstage? Were their legs wobbly, and did their heads feel like jelly?

One by one, the other fifth-graders paraded up onstage, read their lines, and marched off. Finally, Ms. Kantor called Natalie up.

"What part are you trying out for?"

"Peter Pan," Natalie said loudly.

Brianna smirked. "Poor thing."

Natalie was not in costume. She was wearing her jeans and a white sweatshirt with mysterious purple stains. For once, the stains were not from her chemistry experiments but from a laundry mistake her father had made.

Ms. Bunder handed Natalie the script. For a moment, Natalie stood perfectly still. Then slowly she began to move.

Abby stared at her in amazement. For a girl who hated sports, Natalie was incredibly graceful. Why had she never noticed it before?

After a moment, she forgot that she was watching her friend. She was seeing Peter Pan move and think and feel.

When Natalie finished, there was a moment of silence. Then everyone began to applaud. Except for Brianna, who sat frowning at Natalie.

"Is this the role you really want?" Ms. Bunder asked in a quiet voice.

Natalie shrugged. "Yes, I guess so."

Ms. Bunder and Ms. Kantor both wrote a few notes on their papers. Then they stood up. The auditions were over.

"Ms. Kantor and I are going to spend the next

hour discussing what we just saw. You've all done a great job, and we have some hard decisions in front of us," Ms. Bunder said. "We can't tell you anything now, so go home and get some rest. Ms. Kantor will announce the results tomorrow."

Chapter 11

Friday

"No news is good news."

Cube of Quotes Calendar

Is this true or not? If Ms. Kantor's class didn't have news, we'd go crazy. Now that we finally have it, we're still crazy.

The class is in an uproar—at least some of it. I don't know how I feel.

This morning we all got to school early. When the bell rang, the entire class hurried to Ms. Kantor's classroom. Ms. Kantor was sitting at her desk, grading papers.

"What roles did we get?" Zach asked. "Am I Captain Hook?"

"Take off your coat, Zach, and sit down quietly at your desk. Then we'll talk about the play."

"We've waited since yesterday to hear!" Bethany wailed.

Ms. Kantor nodded. "I know you're impatient. However, we have to wait until everyone is here."

We all had our coats and boots and scarves off in record time. (Will make <u>Hayes Book of World Records</u> as Fastest Fifth-Grade Dash to Desks.)

The last person straggled in. We rose for the pledge. Then we sat down. Ms. Kantor took the roll call. (We wanted another kind of role call.) Then she collected our homework.

(Note: Put in <u>Hayes Book of World Records</u> as Slowest, Most Agonizing Wait.)

When Ms. Kantor finally picked up her notebook and said it was time to tell us which roles we would play in <u>Peter Pan</u>, the whole class breathed a sigh of relief. Or was it a sigh of anxiety?

Brianna fluffed her hair.

Natalie was reading a Harry Potter book under her desk and didn't look up.

I crossed my fingers and rubbed Alex's good luck teddy bear key chain once more for luck.

Then Ms. Kantor made a speech about "how many talented students we have in this class, and how difficult a decision Ms. Bunder and I had."

"Translation," I whispered to Jessica and Natalie, "a lot of people didn't get the parts they wanted."

Natalie shrugged as if she didn't care. Jessica said, "Don't worry."

Finally, Ms. Kantor read the list.

Peter Pan Parts
(Note: Could this be tongue twister? "Playing a part in the Peter Pan production, Polly put a pint of potatoes in the pot."

Another note: Get back to main subject. Even if you don't want to.)

Most Exciting News: Natalie is Peter Pan!

Hooray! Hooray! She looked really happy.

Most Infuriating (but not Most Surprising) News: Brianna is Wendy.

Most Surprising (but not at all Infuriating) News: Jessica is the Crocodile.

Predictable News: Zach is Captain Hook; Tyler is Smee; Bethany is Tinkerbell.

Other News: Rachel and Jon are Mrs. and Mr. Darling. Meghan will be Nana, the nursemaid dog.

Most Shocking News: I will not be onstage at all.

I am not Wendy, Tinkerbell, Peter Pan, Captain Hook, Smee, Mrs. Darling, Michael, John, or even a Lost Boy.

I am the Narrator. I will also do sound effects for Tinkerbell and the Crocodile, who don't speak, but ring and tick instead.

All my dreams are shattered. I am not going to be a star.

Is it because I didn't have acting and singing lessons? I

don't think so. Natalie didn't have lessons, either.

Did Alex's good luck teddy bear chain fail? I don't think so. (But will give it back just in case.)

Was all my rehearsing and practicing for nothing? Don't want to think about it.

Now I have to face my family. They will all be eager to hear how I did. Don't want their a) sympathy, b) pity, or c) comforting words. Don't want to have Isabel tell me I should have breathed deeper, harder, and longer.

Grandma Emma won't see me onstage in a starring role!

Jessica says that the Narrator is very important. She said she's glad I'm doing the sound effects for the Crocodile.

Natalie sympathetic. Offered me half of her favorite dessert. Said that I had done a great audition, and she wished I had won the role of Wendy instead of Brianna.

Brianna not happy, either. "You didn't tell me you'd studied acting," she accused Natalie. "That's not fair!"

She didn't believe Natalie hadn't been taking acting classes.

A group of Brianna's friends went up to Ms. Kantor.

this is an injustice!

"Brianna should be Peter Pan," Bethany announced. "She's practically a professional! This is an injustice!"

"The role of Wendy is a major role," Ms. Kantor observed. "If Brianna doesn't like it, she can always be a pirate or a Lost Boy."

"Don't worry about me!" Brianna said quickly. "I accept the role of Wendy. The play must go on!"

Brianna got a starring role. My role is minor. The play could easily go on without me.

Chapter 12

Friday | after school

"A hard beginning makes a good ending."

—John Heywood

Pocket Proverb Calendar

That's for sure! Especially today. See below for details.

At the end of the day, Ms. Kantor called me up to her desk.

"I know you're disappointed, Abby," she said. "You did a very good reading for the part of Wendy; however, Ms. Bunder and I have an important job for you."

Then Ms. Kantor told me what she and Ms. Bunder wanted me to do.

"The play is old-fashioned, and some of

it is outdated," Ms. Kantor said. "We want you to rewrite it."

"Me?" I said.

"We noticed during the audition that you made changes to Wendy's lines as you were reading."

"Oops," I said.

"We liked the changes," she said. "We wondered if you wanted to do more. Ms. Bunder thinks that you'll do a great job. I agree. What do you say?"

"Yes!" I cried, before the news had even sunk in.

She told me that I could take the script home this weekend.

"I know the play inside and out," I told her. "I've rehearsed it, read it, sung it, danced it, watched it, and dreamed about it."

"Then you'll be able to get right to work," Ms. Kantor said.

"Do I have to have it all done by next week?"

Ms. Kantor reassured me. "Just get a

few ideas together. You'll be working on it with Ms. Bunder. You'll meet after school to discuss the changes."

Ms. Kantor gave me Ms. Bunder's phone number and told me to call her to discuss the play.

Yippee! Hooray! Zippety-do-dah! I WILL BE WORKING ON THE PLAY WITH MS. BUN-DER. Can things get any better?

Yes. I could have a part in the play, too.

This <u>almost</u> makes up for not having a starring role.

Chapter 13

So does Peter Pan.
That's all I can write today. ByeIII

Busy, busy, busy, busy, busy, busy, busy.

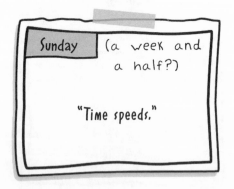

Sunday   (a week and
a half?)

"Time speeds."

Dear Journal,
Please don't feel neglected. I still
love you. But today I have to
paint scenery and help with costumes.
Love, your best friend Abby

Wednesday

"Time gallops."

I am so busy writing, I don't have a
chance to write!

Chapter 14

Monday | Grandma Emma is Coming Today!

"Everything happens to everybody sooner or later if there is time enough."
— *George Bernard Shaw*
Baby Ballerina Calendar

What has happened over the last five weeks:

(Everything).

Number of rehearsals Ms. Kantor's class has had: 22 including 2 dress rehearsals

Rehearsals that took place during recess: 20

Number of kids who complained about missing recess: No one, because everyone wanted to be in the play.

Times Zach got carried away and menaced other kids with his hook: 5

Boasts and brags Natalie has made about having the lead role: 0

Boasts and brags Brianna has made about her costume and dancing, singing, and acting abilities: 1,000,000,000,000

Number of times Ms. Kantor said, "Thank you, Brianna, we are not on Broadway": 75

Number of kids and parents it took to make and paint the sets: 36 people over 2 days

What Ms. Bunder and I did to the script:

Made Peter Pan less boastful.

Changed a lot of the words so they sounded less old-fashioned.

Turned the Indians into space aliens, who try to kidnap Wendy and bring her onto their space shuttle.

Put in a lot more jokes.

What else I've done:
Painted sets.

Last Saturday, the whole class got together to paint an ocean with fish, a spaceship for the aliens, and tropical trees for Mermaid Island. Jessica and I painted Nana's doghouse bright blue. Then we helped Natalie make waves (ha-ha).

And I've also:
Sewn costumes (sort of).
Learned to play a xylophone for the voice of Tinkerbell.
Figured out how to use a metronome for crocodile ticktock.

Abby flung open the front door and threw down her backpack. "I'm home! Where's Grandma Emma?"

She ran down the hallway and into the kitchen. Her father and grandmother were sitting at the kitchen table in front of mugs of coffee and a plate of cookies.

"My baby!" Grandma Emma opened her arms and drew Abby into a big hug. She was short and slim, with curly white hair that had once been red and wild. She wore a blue suit jacket over a black turtleneck sweater and jeans.

"Grandma, I'm not a baby!" Abby said. "I'm in fifth grade. Some of the girls in my class already have pierced ears." She shot a meaningful look at her father. "If my parents weren't so old-fashioned, I would, too."

"It's just that we spent so much time together when you were a baby," Grandma Emma sighed. "I still miss seeing you all the time."

"Me, too!" Abby exclaimed. "I wish I was cousin Cleo and lived near you."

Grandma Emma gave her another hug. "I wish you did, too. I also wish you could get to know cousin Cleo. How long has it been since you've seen her?"

"Five years." Abby took a cookie from the plate and popped it in her mouth. She envied cousin Cleo, who got to spend so much time with her grandmother. She hoped Grandma Emma didn't love cousin Cleo more than she loved her. Wasn't there a saying that absence makes the heart grow fonder?

"You've grown," her grandmother said affectionately, looking her over. "That's a standard grandmotherly comment, isn't it?"

Paul Hayes smiled. "We would be disappointed if you didn't say it."

"You're becoming a lovely young woman," Grandma Emma commented.

Her father nodded his head. "I agree."

"Who, me?" Abby tried to remember what she had looked like in the mirror that morning. Nothing special, certainly. Just the usual nose, mouth, and eyes. Add in the unusual hair, and that about summed it up.

"Abby's been hard at work on the play," Paul Hayes said.

"It's tomorrow night, isn't it?" Grandma Emma sipped her coffee. "How exciting! I can't wait to see it!"

"I'm just the Narrator," Abby apologized. "It isn't much of a part. One of my best friends is Peter Pan."

"The little roles are as important as the big ones," her grandmother said. "No one can be on a stage all by themselves."

"You've never met Brianna!" Abby exclaimed. Still, her grandmother's words gave her a warm feeling inside.

"It's not what you are, it's who you are," Grandma Emma concluded. She rummaged in her bag and handed Abby a wrapped package. It was flat and square and light.

Abby opened it carefully. She had already guessed what it was. "Salt and Pepper Shakers of North America Calendar," she said. "Just what I've always wanted!"

Her grandmother nodded. "I wanted to remind you of me."

"I always think of you whenever I put salt and pepper on my food," Abby said.

"Because I'm so peppery?" Grandma Emma joked.

Her father laughed. "Is this like the fairy tale where the daughter tells her father she loves him as much as salt?"

"No, it's because of Grandma Emma's salt and pepper shaker collection!" Abby jiggled the salt shaker in the middle of the table. It was shaped like a mouse. The pepper shaker was shaped like a cat. They had been a present from Grandma Emma. "Now I'll think of Grandma Emma whenever I look at the calendar."

Abby gave her grandmother a kiss. "I have a present for you, too." She pulled Grandma Emma's Island from her backpack. She had had it matted and framed. Now it looked almost like a real piece of art.

"An island! For me!" her grandmother exclaimed.

"No one's ever given me an island before! Thank you, Abby!"

The front door slammed. Quarreling voices were heard in the hallway.

"Sounds like the twins," Abby's father said. "I knew the peace wouldn't last long."

"Hello, Isabel! Hello, Eva!" Grandma Emma called.

Abby's two older sisters burst through the door. As usual they were glowering at each other. The Twin Truce had been forgotten.

"Now, what are you two arguing about today?" Grandma Emma asked.

"Which would you rather do first?" Eva said. "Go to my games or watch Isabel debate?"

Grandma Emma gave them each a hug and a kiss. "First on my list is to rest from my trip," she announced. "Then I'm going to see Abby in her play. After that, I'm up for grabs. I plan to spend time with each of you."

Paul Hayes stood up and grabbed his car keys from a hook on the wall. "I have to pick up Alex from his swim lesson," he said. "We'll be back in twenty minutes."

Isabel took a cookie from the plate. "Did you make these?" she asked Grandma Emma.

"No, they're direct from the bakery. What's the latest in fingernail polish?" she asked.

As Isabel spread out her fingers for Grandma Emma to admire, Eva sniffed in disapproval.

"How about you, Eva? Any new sports? Let's see — you swim, run, and play basketball, lacrosse, and softball. What else?"

"Skiing and ice-skating," Eva said. "Do you want to come with me?"

"I love to ice-skate," Grandma Emma said. "Do they rent skates at the rink?"

Abby leafed through the pages of her new calendar. It was good to have her grandmother here. Everyone was happy. Even the twins had simmered down to an occasional annoyed murmur.

Chapter 15

Tuesday

"Reach for the stars."

Working Woman's Wisdom Calender
(As quoted by Olivia Hayes)

Yes, my mother said it <u>again</u> this morning! Well, I reached for them and wasn't tall enough to touch them. So I have to settle for watching the stars.

The stars are Zach, Tyler, Brianna, and Natalie. They will do a good job of acting tonight. All hope is not dead for me. I am only ten years old. Maybe someday, when I'm older, I will be the star of a tragedy. (Have had good practice with <u>Peter Pan</u>.)

Grandma Emma taught me to make envelopes last night. I made a stack of them

from Alex's nature magazines. I
now have monkey, lynx, cheetah,
antelope, spotted lizard,
grasshopper, dung beetle, spider,
eagle, copperhead snake, and
blue heron envelopes. Gave a
few to Alex so he wouldn't be
mad I tore up his old magazines. (He
doesn't read them anymore but says he
does.)

The doorbell is ringing. It's Jessica, come
to pick me up for school. She wants to say
hi to Grandma Emma. Have to go! Wish me
luck!

Half an hour before the performance was due to
start, Abby stood on the stage and surveyed the gym.
It had been transformed. All the chairs had been
taken off the stage and were lined up in rows. Now
they stood waiting for the people who were going to
fill them. It made Abby dizzy to think of all the people who would be here tonight — not just her family
and her friends' families, but neighbors, teachers,
kids, families from other grades, and the school

principal. There might be hundreds of people watching!

Backstage, Ms. Kantor bustled around, fixing costumes, soothing tempers, reassuring nervous actors, and telling others to settle down.

The aliens struggled into their shiny costumes. When they walked, silver bug antennae wiggled on their heads. The pirates adjusted colorful bandannas, while Zach, who wore all black, tugged on a pair of boots he had borrowed from an older brother.

"Look at Tinkerbell," Jessica whispered to Abby.

Bethany wore a pink-and-white tutu, with pink tights and ballet slippers. She had a glittery crown on her head and a silver wand in her hand.

She rose on her toes and twirled around the stage. "Don't forget to announce my entrance," she said to Abby.

"I won't!" Abby held up the xylophone stick. "It'll be loud and clear."

"Where's Wendy?" Ms. Bunder had an armful of scripts. "Has anyone seen her yet?"

"I'm here!" Brianna stepped out from behind the curtain. As Wendy, she was wearing a long pale-blue silk nightgown with panels of lace at the cuffs and neckline and matching ballet slippers. Her long dark hair streamed down around her shoulders.

"Does she wear that thing to bed?" Abby whispered to Jessica. "I thought she'd be wearing flannel jammies and bunny slippers. Or boxers and a T-shirt."

"My entire family is here tonight," Brianna announced. "Parents, younger sister, all my grandparents, two great-grandparents, twelve cousins, and four sets of aunts and uncles. Plus my neighbors and my mother's office friends. They've all come to see me perform."

"She could fill the gym all by herself," Abby murmured.

"Brianna, I have some small script changes to go over with you," Ms. Bunder said.

"Of course. I'm a professional," Brianna said.

Natalie adjusted a feather in her hat. It had been hard finding a green hat for her, but Abby had finally unearthed one in her sister Isabel's closet.

"Are you ready, Peter Pan?" Ms. Kantor asked. She was carrying a large felt crocodile head.

Natalie nodded.

"Are you nervous?"

"A little," Natalie admitted, "but I've got my lucky socks on."

"Lucky socks! I want a pair!" Ms. Kantor motioned to Jessica. "Can you put this crocodile head on by yourself or do you need help?"

"I need help," Jessica said.

Tyler peeked between the curtains. "People are starting to come in."

"You're on first, Abby," Ms. Kantor said. She fitted the crocodile mask over Jessica's head. "Do you want to review your lines one last time?"

Abby took a deep breath. She had written most of her own lines and then memorized them, but for a moment her mind went blank. She glanced at the script, then touched the new silver snowflake necklace that Grandma Emma had given her.

Ten minutes later, the lights flickered, then darkened. The hum of voices quieted. Abby stepped onstage in front of a packed gym.

When she sat down again, only a few minutes later, she hadn't forgotten her lines, tripped, stumbled, said the wrong word, or stared dumbly at the audience. Other than that, she wasn't sure how she had done. Everyone had applauded enthusiastically, but that didn't mean anything. After all, she was the first one onstage. The audience was probably glad the play had started.

"You were great," Jessica whispered from inside her crocodile costume.

"Do you mean it?" Her heart was still pounding wildly.

"A crocodile wouldn't lie!"

Abby picked up the xylophone and metronome and went to her seat in front of the stage to wait for Tinkerbell's entrance.

In the moments when Tinkerbell or the Crocodile were not onstage, Abby watched the play. No one forgot lines, and the fifth-graders acted their parts with energy and enthusiasm. The audience was enjoying it, too. When the aliens came onstage with their spacecraft lit up by a strobe light, everyone burst into applause.

Every now and then, Abby glanced into the audience. Her grandmother was watching with a huge smile on her face. Neither Isabel nor Eva seemed bored. Alex, her seven-year-old brother, was manning the camcorder, with her father right behind him. Alex knew how to operate the thing, but who knew what a seven-year-old behind a camcorder might do. He might zoom in on everyone's feet or decide to film the play sideways.

Finally, Captain Hook fell into the water where the Crocodile awaited him. The three Darling children returned to their home, where they were reunited with their parents and Nana.

The curtain fell. The audience went wild. They yelled, cheered, whistled, and stamped their feet, as one by one the players came out onstage for the curtain call.

Finally, the entire cast stood onstage in a semicircle. Ms. Kantor and Ms. Bunder joined them, to more applause.

When the cheering died down, the teachers came forward.

Ms. Kantor cleared her throat. "We'd like to acknowledge someone who made a very special contribution to the play," she said.

Who was that, Abby wondered. Brianna? Natalie? She hoped it wasn't Brianna. The acknowledgment would take a minute, but the bragging would go on for months.

"A fifth-grade student rewrote the entire script of *Peter Pan*. We think she did a great job. We'd like her to come forward now."

"Me?" Abby said. "You're talking about me?"

"Yes, you!" Jessica gave her a friendly shove.

She stumbled toward the front of the stage, where her teachers put their arms around her.

"This is Abby Hayes," Ms. Bunder introduced her. "Let's give her a round of applause. She wrote the very entertaining and lively version of *Peter Pan* that was performed tonight."

The audience rose to its feet. Cheering loudest of all were her parents, grandmother, and siblings. They looked proud and thrilled. Abby waved to them and beamed. Maybe she was a star, after all.

Chapter 16

Tuesday	(night, after the play)

I don't need any inspiring quotes tonight. I am floating on cloud nine! Or maybe it's cloud ninety!

cloud #9

Standing ovations
Brianna got: 3
Standing ovations
Natalie got: 4 (Ha-ha ha-ha!)
Total strangers who stopped to give me compliments on the script: 32
Cookies Tyler and Zach gobbled at the cast party afterward: 25 each (I counted)

Flavors of punch Bethany spilled on her pink tutu: grape and tutti-frutti

Number of times Eva asked me to do her creative-writing homework for her: about 6

NEWS FLASH!

There were many surprised parents in the  audience tonight. Among them were the Hayes parents, Paul and Olivia. They regarded their daughter with awe and respect and said (with a touch of reproach), "Why didn't you tell us you were rewriting the script?"

Abby Hayes told them she wanted to surprise them. She also didn't want to disappoint them.

They were not disappointed. They said to Abby that it was one of the best school productions they had ever seen.

Natalie's parents were also shocked and stunned at their daughter's talent. They announced, in public, that they would enroll Natalie in acting classes immediately.

"Instead of basketball?" Natalie asked quickly.

"You have to do a sport, too," they said.

Natalie was not happy about that but may try to convince them to let her take a dance class instead.

The only adult not surprised by this amazing display of youthful talent was Grandma Emma. She said she knew it all along.

After the cast party, we had a Hayes family party. Hot apple cider, donuts, and tea were enjoyed by all. Isabel and Eva only fought once. Grandma Emma did a jig in the middle of the living room floor. Abby Hayes sang a song from Peter Pan. Alex reviewed the video-cassette of the play with the rest of the family. He did a good job of filming it!

Am very, very, very tired, and my head

feels like a beehive with lots of buzzing inside. Alex just came up to give me his
teddy bear key chain.

"The good luck worked for you," he said.
"You can keep it."

Gave younger brother a hug. Told him I
will use it to try to get parents to agree to
pierced ears.